SHAKEY'S
LOOSE

SHAKEY'S LOOSE

RENAY JACKSON

Frog, Ltd.
Berkeley, California

Published by Frog, Ltd.

Frog, Ltd. books are distributed by
North Atlantic Books
P.O. Box 12327
Berkeley, California 94712

Cover illustrations © 2004 by Ariel Shepard
Cover and book design by Maxine Ressler

Printed in the United States of America

Distributed to the book trade by Publishers Group West

North Atlantic Books' publications are available through most bookstores. For further information, call 800-337-2665 or visit our website at www.northatlanticbooks.com.

Substantial discounts on bulk quantities are available to corporations, professional associations, and other organizations. For details and discount information, contact our special sales department.

Library of Congress Cataloging-in-Publication Data
Jackson, Renay, 1959–
    Shakey's loose / by Renay Jackson.
        p. cm.
    ISBN 1-58394-107-X (pbk.)
    1. Informers—Fiction. 2. Oakland (Calif.)—Fiction. 3. Brothers—Death—Fiction. 4. Ex-convicts—Fiction. 5. Revenge—Fiction.
I. Title.
    PS3610.A3547S53 2004
    813'.6—dc22
                                                    2004017136

    1 2 3 4 5 6 7 8 9   DATA   09 08 07 06 05 04

*Dedicated to
my daughters,
whom I love and cherish.*

OTHER NOVELS BY RENAY JACKSON

Oaktown Devil

Turf War

Peanut's Revenge

Crackhead

In order to
keep a man down ...

You must stay down
with him.

—*Muhammad Ali*

AUTHOR'S NOTE

This book is based totally on the writer's imagination. Any similarities to actual events are purely coincidental. Although many of the locations are real, they were used only to make the story believable.

SHOUts

L.B. AND BARBARA GREEN—YOU TWO SOLD
SO MANY OF MY BOOKS THAT I FIGURE YOU
SHOULD OPEN A BOOKSTORE. THANKS FOR
HELPING OUT.

ALBERTA "BB QUEEN" JACKSON—WHEN YOU
WERE SELECTED GOSPEL GUITARIST OF THE
YEAR, NO ONE WAS PROUDER THAN ME.
GIRL YOU SET A VERY HIGH STANDARD FOR
US TO FOLLOW AND NO MATTER HOW MUCH
SUCCESS I HAVE, I'LL STILL HAVE A MORE
TALENTED SISTER.

TRUE SOLDIERS ONE AND ALL—SHAMBA,
RICKY G., LONZO, C.J.—REST IN PEACE
Y'ALL.

RENDA BELL, SYBIL EVANS, LUTHER MCGILL,
LINDA BARNETT, KAMMIE BARFIELD, AND
MARCEL—THE HEART AND SOUL OF
FREMONT HIGH CLASS OF '77 REUNION
COMMITTEE.

BARBARA KEENAN—YOUR STORE, "A WORLD OF BOOKS" HAS BEEN AND CONTINUES TO BE MY BOOKSTORE HOME. THANKS FOR MAKING ME THE RESIDENT AUTHOR.

THE FRIENDS OF CHESTER HIMES—WOW, AUTHOR OF THE YEAR. THANK YOU GUYS FOR CHOOSING LITTLE OLD ME.

DON WATERS—MAN YOU AND L.B. SHOULD OPEN A PROMOTIONAL COMPANY CAUSE YAW GOT THE GIFT OF GAB.

DARRYL ROSS—MY FELLOW RAP PROMOTER. IT SEEMS LIKE ONLY YESTERDAY THAT WE WERE OUT BUSTING RHYMES.

LAST BUT FIRST—I THANK THE LORD ALMIGHTY BECAUSE WITHOUT GOD, NONE OF THIS IS POSSIBLE.

TABLE OF CONTENTS

PROLOGUE:
THE SKINNY

It was a year when Oaktown seemed to be a personal playground and battlefield for dope dealers. Ever since two of the most notorious pushers in the flatlands were murdered in the preceding months, rival gangs and independent dealers had been fighting for control of the lucrative drug market. Drive-by shootings, execution-style slayings, random murders, and vicious beatings happened daily.

As the city's death count spiraled to record-setting numbers, many unsolved murders were attributed to the drug wars even though, in several cases, drugs had nothing to do with the crime. Several wannabees took their turn trying to control their hood, only to be 187'd (the penal code for murder). Law-abiding citizens lived in fear, hoping they would not be in the wrong place at the wrong time.

Generation X teens were much more violent than the

Baby Boomers. A fistfight to solve a dispute in the '70s would be a shootout in the '90s. These kids, walking around with pants hanging down low on their butts, showing little or no respect, had people afraid to come out at night. Oaktown was quickly gaining a reputation as Murder Capital, U.S.A. Blacks were exiting the city in alarming numbers, heading to newly built tract-home communities in traditional white cities.

The media played it for all it was worth, happy to give the public a daily dose of black-on-black crime. They didn't care that they were showing only one part of Oaktown—the evil. Their job was to sell papers or gain viewers and listeners. Everything was sensationalized to the hilt, with so-called experts explaining what it would take to stop the violence.

Many of these "experts" weren't born or raised there, nor did they live in Oaktown, so they really didn't have a clue as to what they were talking about. Although it would sound good to white people watching the show in the comforts of their suburban home, the majority of blacks knew it was a bunch of bull.

They couldn't possibly understand what it was like to live in a neighborhood where violence lurked around every corner, the community never slept, and the only job attainable was for minimum wage. Add in lack of a decent education, defiance to authority, being second- and third-generation welfare recipients, and you would start to have an idea of the situation.

Politicians jumped on the bandwagon, as they always do in a crisis: demanding immediate action from the police force and threatening the Chief, forming committees to brainstorm ideas, vowing to implement job training programs for minorities, and serving up heaping plates of rhetoric. To the dealers, it didn't matter how many young black men died, only who would emerge as king.

Oaktown had not seen this much bloodshed since the early '80s, when the arrests and subsequent downfall of the three most powerful dealers in the city's history all occurred in the same year. At the time, members of the Oaktown Police Department or OPD were beside themselves, handing out commendations and promotions while declaring the war on drugs a success. They always omit the fact that the gangs' violence among themselves and towards each other plays a pivotal role in eliminating bad boys.

The capture of the big three sparked violence and death throughout the city. Several would-be kingpins were toppled, and no organization could dominate. After a few years, two bonafide leaders emerged from the rubble. One was Ricky "Stoney" Jordan, who wrested control of the city's west side. Alphonse "Tonio" Malone ran the east. The north side, as usual, was free-agent territory dominated by Ghost Town and Dogtown entrepreneurs along with scattered independent dealers.

In 1994, Stoney and Tonio died within three days of each other at the hands of Curtis "Buckey" Jones, a small-time hood with big-time aspirations. Their deaths left a huge void to be filled, and no true leader (if you can call the meanest man in town a leader) to carry on "business as usual." Now, ten years after the violent turf wars of the '80s, Oaktown was on the verge of reliving the terror.

1
FRIENDS AND OUTLAWS

The black Cadillac Fleetwood sped up Lincoln Avenue heading towards the Oaktown Hills. Too $hort's latest hit, "Life is Too $hort," blasted from the sound system, but the four occupants of the car were too deep into their own thoughts to notice.

> *people wanna say - it's just my time*
> *brothers like me - had ta work for mine*
> *eight years on the mike - an i'm not jokin*
> *Sir Too $hort - comin straight from Oakland*

Passing the Mormon Temple, which provided one of the most splendid views of the Bay Area, the driver spoke.

"Lookout Point, Boss?"

"Right, dog, let's see what The Point looks like. If it's occupied, then we go up to Skyline."

"OK, Big Ed."

4

Edward Tatum was the boss. Six foot five, two hundred and eighty pounds of muscle, he was an imposing physical specimen. A former bodyguard for Alphonse Malone's east-side empire, "Big Ed" anointed himself kingpin after the murders of "Tonio" and "Big T," Tonio's personal bodyguard and Big Ed's mentor in cruelty. No one in the organization challenged Big Ed because everyone knew that would be an immediate death sentence. He would kill you without blinking.

A former All City football player and wrestler, Big Ed lost his dream of college ball, like so many others before him, due to lousy grades. Playing a few years of semi-pro for what now amounted to chicken scratch, he realized that road wouldn't make him famous or wealthy. One day, while waiting for his wife to cash her welfare check at Eastmont Mall, he ran into his old wrestling buddy Tonio, now a local dope dealer.

Big Ed was impressed by Tonio's flashy jewelry, fancy ride, and phat bankroll. Seeing those stacks of greenbacks wrapped in rubber bands sold him hook, line, and sinker. He knew instantly how he would provide for his kids. When Tonio offered him a job as enforcer, Big Ed had accepted without a second thought.

Hooking a right at Joaquin Miller Road, the Caddy made a quick left into the gated area leading up to Lookout Point. "The Point," as the flatland boys called it, was no more than a patch of dirt and rocks where maybe ten cars could fit at the max. Teen lovers would park there and make out, and sometimes rich kids held Friday night keg parties.

The Point was unoccupied at the three in the morning.

5

It held a spectacular view. The Bay Bridge gleamed, San Francisco's skyline radiated, and your breath was taken away by Lake Merritt, Oaktown's waterfront, and the Pacific Ocean. However, if you looked immediately down from the Point, all you saw were trees, weeds, and underbrush.

"Pull over right here, Flea," Big Ed barked.

Clyde Featherstone was Big Ed's driver. Five six, one forty, Clyde was a product of the penal institutional system. A career criminal, in and out of jail all his life, Clyde knew nothing but wrong. His mentality was stuck on stupid. A little man, Clyde Featherstone had a big heart. He was loyal to whomever his boss was at the time. The boy wasn't shit—he was an ass-kisser—but still one dangerous individual. Called "Flea" because of his appearance, he was strong as an ox, just small in stature.

Flea was twenty-six but looked forty. All the partying, incarceration, and rough times had done a number on his features. With sideburns down to his jawbone, a Fu Manchu mustache and beard, and pockmarks on his face, he resembled a hairy turtle.

Big Ed was first out of the vehicle, stretching his large frame fully. He wore black Levi 505s, a black form-fitting sweater, gold ropes dangling from his neck, black suede Stacy Adams, and a white straw hat accentuated by a black and gold feather. His peanut butter complexion and clean-shaven face resembled a buffed-out Denzel. Massive hands displayed huge diamond and gold nugget rings.

Hopping out of the back seat of the four-door were Big Ed's henchmen, Billy Ray and Donnie Barnes. Crime followed these two brothers like a bad habit. Billy Ray was the eldest by a year at twenty-seven, but if you saw them side by side, you'd mistakenly consider them to be twins. They both stood six three and weighed two-forty but appeared to be much larger due to all the weightlifting done over the years.

Their facial features were scary. Permanent scratches, large flat noses, protruding foreheads, cream-colored blotched skin, and evil scowls yelled out "danger" to those who saw them for the first time. They dressed the same every day, which was nothing to write home about: blue denim Levi 501s hanging halfway down their butts, white t-shirt, blue checkerboard shirt coat, along with dirty black and red sneakers. Neither man wore gold or frequented barbershops because being well groomed wasn't a part of their makeup.

"Pop the trunk, Flea," Big Ed deadpanned. Flea opened the glove compartment, pushed the trunk release button, then got out and joined the rest of his homeys at the rear of the car. Inside were Alvin Jenkins and Vanessa Harris. Alvin was badly beaten and barely breathing. Their mouths, eyes, ankles, and wrists were duct-taped. Blood lined the bed of the trunk.

Billy Ray pulled Alvin out while Donnie jerked Vanessa like a rag doll. Ripping the tape from their eyes and mouths violently, they slung these two on the ground harder than necessary.

"Where's my money?" Big Ed demanded.

"Big Ed, I told you I'll get it, I just need more time," Alvin pleaded.

"Yo time is up, niggah. Now I'mo give you one mo

chance ta come clean. Where mah goddamn money at?"

"Man, the game done...."

Big Ed's foot to Alvin's mouth stopped his words in mid-sentence. Vanessa's eyes grew big as saucers, not fearing for her man but afraid of what would happen when her interrogation came. Big Ed looked her over then casually asked, "Bitch, where's my money?"

"Big E-E-Ed, I'll give you what we got left, just let us l-l-live," she pleaded, talking as fast as she could.

"Y'all told me I would have sixteen grand in a week, but it took me two weeks to find you. How much you got?"

"I got four G's, d-d-don't know what Alvin got," she stammered.

"Hoe, that's still twelve G's short!" he hollered.

"Big Ed, please, that's all we got. You still come out two thousand ahead."

"How much that sorry-ass nigger of yours got?"

"I don't know, he won't say."

Returning his attention to Alvin, Big Ed continued.

"How much you got, dog?" he inquired nonchalantly.

Alvin was struggling to breathe, since each breath would result in dirt going up his nostrils. The white Italian suit he wore with blue silk shirt and matching kicks looked ragged, even though he'd just purchased it the day before.

"Man, I ain't got shit. So if you gone kill me, you may as well kill me now, then you never will get paid," he said defiantly.

"Al, ain't nobody said shit 'bout killin' you. The subject is money."

"Well, right now, I ain't got it."

Alvin felt as though Big Ed really didn't want to kill him because he wanted money. If he played his cards right by calling Big Ed's bluff, he would gain enough time to get out of town without a trace. But his last remark hit a nerve with Big Ed.

He never saw Big Ed give Billy Ray the eye and a quick nod of the head. Vanessa didn't either. Alvin opened his mouth to speak just as Billy Ray pulled the trigger on the 357 Magnum he always carried.

The shot went directly into Alvin's mouth and blew his tongue off. Billy Ray always carved X's into his bullets so they could explode on impact. The result was just as Billy Ray desired: Alvin's face splattered across the dirt-covered lot and left nothing OPD or the coroner would be able to identify.

As if it were a planned movie script, Donnie pulled a chainsaw out of the trunk, jerked the starter rope, then cut off Alvin's hands. The brothers seemed to enjoy their gruesome tasks. Once finished, they placed the chopped-off fingers, minus his rings, into a ziplock sandwich bag, which they would toss onto "somebodies freeway" where it would be run over repeatedly by the never-ceasing traffic.

Flea took the dead man's wallet, ropes, rings, and everything else in his pockets then went back to the driver's seat to count the money. Billy Ray and Donnie grabbed the remainder of the body by the shoulders and legs, swung it back and forth a few times, then flung it down the hill. As Alvin's body flew through the air, the brothers gave each other the "raise the roof" dance, which with these two resembled a bench-pressing warm-up routine, then returned their focus to Vanessa and Big Ed.

"I-I-I'll give you everything I've g-g-got! Please, Big E-Ed, just don't kill me. I d-d-don't wanna die like this!" Vanessa was hysterical.

"All right, baby, this is what we gonna do. First, we gone go to yo house and you gone pay me. Second, I need to make sho you don't talk. Now you gone hafta tell me how I can trust you enuff fa dat."

"Big Ed, I'll give my word, that's my bond. I ain't gonna say nothin, to NOBODY!" She emphasized the last point.

Big Ed pondered her last statement then spoke. "Somehow, Ms. Vanessa, I believe you." Looking at the gruesome twosome he ordered, "Put her in the back seat. Billy Ray, you ride up front."

The brothers did as told and they all got inside. Flea revved up the engine and let it idle. Vanessa felt like a sardine sandwiched between Big Ed and Donnie in the back seat but was grateful to be still alive.

"Where to, Boss?" Flea asked while reaching over the seat and handing Alvin's possessions to Big Ed.

"Flea, take us to Al and 'Nessa's crib."

"Buckle up, my people," Flea warned.

No one buckled up, as Flea knew they wouldn't; he just liked to say shit like that. It always made him feel important. In the back seat Big Ed told Vanessa to lean forward, then began unwrapping the duct tape from her wrists and ankles. While gently freeing her legs, he became aroused because Vanessa Harris was phine.

She was five foot eight, one hundred and fifty pounds,

and yellow as buttered popcorn. The girl had a 36-24-36 frame with full pouty lips, curves in all the right places, and very muscular legs. The silk party dress she wore accented her awesome body, and the fact that most of it was torn off left little to the imagination. Big Ed wondered to himself what the hell did she see in Alvin. If it weren't for her, he never would've bought into their scam in the first place.

Big Ed counted the take from Al, which totaled nine hundred in cash. The rings and ropes were cheaper than anything he would wear, so he gave that stuff to Flea, Billy Ray, and Donnie, along with three hundred dollars each. Empty-handed, he began his speech:

"Friends helping muthafuckin friends. What it was was friends cheatin friends. You muthafuckas played me because I trusted you. Once I went to that got-dam party that you called a meetin and saw fools I ain't seen in fifteen years with papers in dey hands, I tole yaw I wanted my money back."

As Big Ed spoke a cold chill ran through Vanessa's body.

"What y'all say? 'Big Ed, it's just gone take a little mo time.' All the while y'all spending money like it's goin outta style. Then to top it off, you start hidin from me."

Vanessa was afraid to move. She attempted to speak but no sound came out. Her vocal cords betrayed her when she needed them most. She'd warned Alvin not to accept Big Ed's money because he had a reputation for killing people.

"Friends Helping Friends" was the latest version of the decades-old "Pyramid" scheme. On paper you had fifteen squares, eight on the bottom row, four above that, two, then one. Whoever's name was in the top square was labeled the President/Chair-person and would receive the two-thousand-dollar entry fee from each of the eight people starting at the bottom. Once paid, the President was no longer in the game because his or her initial two-grand investment had increased to sixteen.

Now the Gameboard split down the middle, with the two Vice-President squares occupying Presidential spots on their own board, along with eight blank spots at the bottom, which they would have to recruit new members to fill, thus collecting their payoff. When people like Big Ed entered the game it spelled trouble because they wouldn't recruit new members. This resulted in the President holding nothing more than a sheet of paper with names on it of people who had given up two grand.

The Caddy streaked down the two-lane Warren Free-way, moving further away from the hills until it merged with the MacArthur. As Flea blended in with the flow of traffic on 580, Billy Ray pushed the down button on the front passenger side window and casually tossed out the sandwich bag. Donnie peered through the back window and smiled as car after car smashed Alvin's hands into mush. Exiting at Ninety-Eighth Avenue, Flea hooked a left and shot past the Knowland Park Zoo and up Golf Links Road. Once he reached Alvin and Vanessa's condominium he pulled into the driveway then asked Vanessa, "What's the security gate code, Boo?"

"Three-one-two," Vanessa responded timidly.

"Which stall?"

"One-two-six."

Parking in stall one-twenty-six, Flea put the gear in park and killed the ignition. Big Ed and Vanessa got out, then he told his flunkies before their feet hit the ground, "Y'all wait right here."

Flea pulled three hot beers from under the seat, passed one each to his homeys, then lit up a phat blunt. As Big Ed and Vanessa disappeared into darkness, they reclined in their seats and began their usual pastime: getting stoned and bragging to each other about what they would do with their loot.

2
TIME SERVED

The wrought-iron gates to San Quentin Penitentiary opened slowly, creaking with each movement. To the inmates being released, this was music to their ears. Happy faces awaited them, even though most prisoners were destined to return within a year. The prospects of finding employment were slim enough without the ex-con label they now carried. Most would return to the same old neighborhoods, get with the same friends, and do the same illegal things. The end result would be a return ticket to the big house.

The guards stood at attention with knowing smirks on their faces. They had seen it time and time again. A fool gets out, does something stupid, and comes right back. For many, the realization that their woman had chosen another man during their absence would be all it took to push them over the edge. Others would commit crimes, sell dope, or violate their parole. Whatever the reason, they would return. Of this the Man was sure.

Calvin Jones walked out slowly, taking in the fresh air, which seemed so much better on the outside of the prison walls. "Shakey," as he was called by almost everyone who knew him, felt relieved. Not only was his body in tip-top shape from daily exercise and weight-lifting, but his mind was clear, having spent the past year soul-searching and meditating. While incarcerated, he'd had plenty of time to devise a plan.

First, he would shack up with Nadine because she was the one person who'd stuck by him through thick and thin. He didn't love her but she loved him, and felt like in time, she would grow on him. Shakey was just using her to get to the woman he truly loved, his soon-to-be remarried ex-wife Cassandra.

Second, he would register with his parole officer. This way the Man couldn't give him a one-way ticket back to Quentin on a bullshit charge. Shakey had seen too many brothers locked up for violating their parole—he would not be one of them. In his mind they were stupid. All they had to do was make weekly visits and fool some idiot into thinking they were on the right track. The parole officers were government employees who didn't give a damn about the cons they were paid to help rehabilitate. They were just drawing paychecks and filing paperwork. After you made about four or five visits, they cancelled most future appointments anyway.

Third, he would try to find work by registering with the Unemployment Office, or EDD, as it was called. He also had a line on a construction job through one of his prison contacts. Oaktown had rebuilt City Hall and signed contracts to construct two more city facilities. In addition, a state building was being erected, a practice site for the local basketball team was being built in the heart of town along with renovating the Arena, the football team was remodeling the stadium, and a major college had just relocated its administrative offices to 11th & Broadway. Oaktown was booming growth-wise, so Shakey felt like his prospects were good.

In many of the contracts awarded, the city placed a stipulation requiring the companies to hire Oaktown residents first or to hire specific percentages of minorities and women. The white-owned companies rarely complied, but Shakey didn't know that. In his mind, since there were plenty of jobs to go around, he would get one. Shakey was in for a rude awakening. No white man in his right mind would consider hiring a black ex-convict and handing him a power tool.

Last but definitely not least, Shakey planned to take Cassandra back from some square named Rainbow. That was the same punk who had caused his little brother Buckey and his sister-in-law Violet to kill each other after being tracked down like dogs by the Man. None of that would have happened if Rainbow hadn't spilled his guts to the Five-O.

When Nadine spotted Shakey coming through the gate, she called out his name then waited patiently like a schoolgirl while he said goodbye to his homeys. He took his time, wishing all his boys well and telling them that they would never see him in jail again. Dressed in the same blue sweatsuit he had on when arrested, along with a white t-shirt and blue tennis shoes, he felt funny. His sweatsuit didn't fit, now that all the weightlifting along with meat-and-potato meals had bulked up his six-foot-one frame tremendously. The sweatsuit was so tight that one wrong move would cause it to burst at the seams. Thick cornrows adorned his scalp, courtesy of one of his jailhouse friends.

Nadine McCoy wore a red knit dress that hugged every inch of her frame. Standing five foot eight, she appeared two inches taller than that because of her red high-heel shoes. The cool October air caused the nipples on her baseball-sized breasts to stand at attention. She had wide hips and a very big behind, which were prominently displayed by her outfit.

She'd gone to Sherry's on MacArthur that morning to get her gold hair fingerwaved, so it was whipped. Rings and ropes adorned her fingers but they were all cubic zirconia. She wore no stockings but Shakey didn't care because her skinny hairy legs looked delicious. After spending a year in the pen, he thought those legs may as well have been Tina's.

As Shakey eagerly walked in her direction he noticed the changes in her appearance. The overlapping belly she always had was gone, and so was the rash on her ears that came from wearing cheap earrings. Her yellow skin tone along with candy-apple red lipstick and nose ring complimented her "sassy" look. Nadine had been on a strict diet and exercise regimen during the last six months. She wanted to look good for her "man," not caring that his heart belonged to another woman. Shakey bear-hugged her, giving her a hungry kiss. His departing homeboys looked on with envy, most of whom had family members picking them up.

"That's what I call a welcoming committee," he said.

"Baby, it's so good to know you're free," she giggled.

"Come on, let's get the hell outta here."

"OK—are you hungry?"

"Naw, just tired, I couldn't sleep last night."

"It's called anticipation, honey."

Look at you, girl—you look good! What you been doin?" he asked while gazing at her physique.

"Fixin myself up for you, baby!" They kissed again.

Shakey couldn't believe what he saw. Nadine looked *good.* He was expecting her to appear as she always did, "toe up like throw-up from the flow up," but she fooled him. In his wildest imagination he would never have expected her to look like this. They got in the car with him on the driver's side and her handing over the keys, even though his license had expired.

The car was a burgundy 1990 Camaro Z-28 with matching velour interior. It was also equipped with spoiler on the back, bra on the hood, jet-black tires, and shiny mag rims. When Nadine got in, her dress slid up to her hips. She didn't attempt to pull it down because she wanted Shakey to notice.

She was parked in front of the hospitality house, so he made a U-turn and cruised away from the house of hell. The two-lane road had the bay to the right, houses where prison employees lived on the left, and trees lining both sides. It was a serene sight to those leaving or visiting, but for the ones headed for incarceration, it was their last glimpse of freedom.

Shakey hit the freeway and got on the McCarthy, commonly known as the San Rafael Bridge, not aware of the fact that his eyes constantly shot glances at Nadine's thighs. She enjoyed the attention he was giving, happy that all her workouts at the gym were well worth the money spent.

"So what's been goin on?" he asked while stroking her legs.

"Not a lot, baby. Cassandra's supposed to be marrying that ass she met named Rainbow. You know she moved in with him?"

"Naw, I didn't know that."

"Well, she did, but that's water under the bridge because I intend to make you forget about her."

"Oh, you do?" he inquired curiously.

"Yes, dear, I do," she stated matter-of-factly.

"What about my kids?"

"They moved in with Rainbow, too."

"When did this take place?"

"It happened last week. I didn't tell you because I didn't want you getting all upset about something you had no control over."

Shakey's grip on the steering wheel got tighter as Nadine talked. She noticed and became quiet, hoping that he would somehow accept the fact that Cassandra was history. As he drove past the brown Chevron Oil refinery vats on the Richmond side of the San Rafael Bridge, he thought about how he and Cassandra were once deeply in love. He knew that he never should have beaten her, but all the nagging about money and getting a job put his nerves on edge. He regretted taking it out on her with violence, but in his mind she'd asked for it. The shock came when she pressed charges, causing him to spend a year in jail.

He took the 23rd Street off ramp, hooked a left, went to Cutting Boulevard and turned right, then headed for his mother's house. Richmond's Easter Hill projects were located on the outskirts of the south side of town. All the units looked the same, which wasn't saying much. They resembled military housing, with many of them boarded up for "maintenance." Tenants had to relocate from one unit to another while maintenance (which consisted of painting inside and out, and laying down fresh carpet and tile) was being done on their place. The sidewalks were rounded off so when you parked, your vehicle would be tilted with only half of it in the streets.

Situated on a man-made hill surrounded by flatlands, Easter Hill was nicknamed "The Rock" due to the fact that big boulders were prominently displayed on every corner and throughout the projects. There were nearly as many traffic bumps, installed to prevent the daily speeding of cars on the narrow streets.

Sarah Jones had been in a deep depression for the last year. It all started when her oldest son Calvin was sentenced to a year in prison for beating on his ex-wife Cassandra. Next, her middle son Curtis died in a shootout with his woman Violet. Then, her only daughter Charlene married her childhood sweetheart Jesse and moved out to begin her own life. To top it off, her baby boy Clarence was convicted to ninety-nine years in prison for murdering three drug dealers in a botched robbery attempt; he had been shipped off to Pelican Bay Penitentiary, where he would languish until his death.

Pelican Bay was located up north near the California/Oregon border. Along with Corcoran Prison down south, it housed the state's most violent offenders. Complaints about guards' abuse and unexplained deaths occurred all the time. No one seemed to care because by the time you reached Pelican Bay or Corcoran, you were deemed "rotten to the core."

Alone for the first time in her life, Sarah had not felt this way since her husband Cleophus was shot dead in bed with another woman. The woman's husband came home unexpectedly, found them together, then killed them both. After pleading temporary insanity, the man was sentenced to only two years in jail.

Sarah stood five foot eight and weighed around one-seventy. Her once-muscular frame had turned into flab during her golden years. A public-aid recipient her entire life, Sarah used the system like many other welfare moms, collecting AFDC, Food Stamps, and Section 8 housing for more than twenty years. She started playing "151"—which is a black expression for crazy—when Clarence turned sixteen. By the time he was eighteen and her welfare checks stopped coming, her disability checks kicked in.

Throughout the projects, the Joneses were known and

feared as one of the craziest families in the ghetto. When her husband was alive, Sarah and Cleo were at each other's throat on a daily basis, and when the police showed up, they would turn on them.

Friends, enemies, strangers, it didn't matter—once Sarah and Cleo started hitting the Old English (which was daily), everybody was fair game. Violence was the only way of life they knew. Their children were chips off the old block, growing up to be just as violent and crazy as their parents.

Sarah heard a car pull up outside, and as was her custom, she went to the window to see who it was. She was momentarily frozen in her tracks by the sight. Her oldest boy Shakey was getting out of the car. Adjusting her muumuu and brushing her hair back with her hands, she rushed out the door.

"Thank you, Lord, you done brought my son home!" she squealed.

"Mama, you know they cain't keep a playa down!" he boasted.

"Boy, come give yo mammy a hug." They embraced lovingly.

"Mama, this is my honey Nadine. Nadine, this is my moms."

"Call me Sarah, baby." They held hands.

"It's so nice to finally meet you," Nadine responded.

"Come on y'all, let's go in the house. I don't need these nosy folks round here knowing my business," Sarah said.

"Who cares, they thank we crazy anyway!" Shakey was all teeth.

Sarah led the way through the front door. Shakey sprawled

out on her sofa while Nadine stood paralyzed in her tracks. The cream-colored carpet was black with filth, walls were dirty, and musty clothes were strewn all over the floor. There was a strong aroma of funk permeating throughout the apartment, and the kitchen resembled a disaster zone. Nadine felt nauseated and asked to use the bathroom.

"It's right up the stairs, baby," Sarah informed her.

Nadine rushed up the stairs to the bathroom and closed the door. When she turned around and saw baby roaches running around the sink, no soap or towels, dirt rings in the tub, and dried-up shit in the toilet, she felt even more nauseated. If she had eaten anything at all that morning it would have come out right then and there. She regained her composure and after flushing the toilet, headed back downstairs.

"Baby, I need to run to the store," Nadine said to Shakey.

"Wait a minute, I'll go with you," he responded.

"No, you stay and visit your mom. I'll be back in about an hour."

"An hour?" he arched his brow.

"Well, I figure since I'm out here in Richmond, I'll drop by my Aunt Dee's house. She lives on Twentieth and Potrero."

"OK, you go visit your Auntie and I'll stay with mom, then you come back and get me."

"OK," she said.

"Wait a minute, honey—brang me two forty-ounce bottles of Old English." Sarah reached into her bosom and pulled out a wrinkled-up five-dollar bill.

"It's alright, Miss Jones. I'll get it for you."

"Honey, call me Sarah."

"I'll get it for you, Sarah—you want something, Shakey?"

"Only you, dear."

Nadine and Sarah both blushed. Nadine walked out the door and was relieved to have fresh air hit her in the face. Then and there, she knew she would not be visiting Sarah's house again. Once she started up the engine, Shakey ran out to the car and got in.

"Baby, what are you doing?"

"Moms thinks I should be with you," he answered.

"What about her beer?"

"Let's go get her the beer, then go to your place."

"Your home," she corrected.

"OK, let's go get the beer, then go home."

They both laughed as Nadine eased away from the curb.

WHATEVER IT
TAKES

As they approached her condominium, Big Ed wrapped his arm around Vanessa's shoulder and whispered in her ear, "Don't try no funny stuff."

"I told you I just want to live," she responded.

"You never know," he said.

"Baby, with me you have nothing to worry about."

She was shaking like a leaf. All of a sudden it was cold, but his thick arm around her shoulder and beefy paws groping her partially exposed breasts warmed her tremendously.

Vanessa had one thing on her mind—doing whatever it took to get Big Ed on her side. She was sure he was going to make a booty call, but if he wanted her, tonight she'd screw the shit out of him. Throughout her entire life, once she figured out how much power her body and looks gave her over men, she used them as weapons. She didn't care that she was their trophy; all that mattered was what she would get out of the arrangement. Tonight she would give the performance of a lifetime because she knew her life depended on it.

Vanessa Harris was a snake, as venomous as they came because she was phine, knew it, and used it to her advantage. She loved Alvin because of his ability to keep her dressed and sporting a phat bankroll. But Alvin was a fool due largely to his inability to recognize danger, and because he liked to flaunt his riches.

None of tonight's happenings would have gone down if he didn't insist that they go to Jimmie's for a night on the town. She told him they should lay low because Big Ed and his henchmen were spreading word around town that they wanted to talk to Al and Ness. Alvin kissed it off as nothing more than veiled threats, but Vanessa took it to heart.

Once at Jimmie's, the couple was unaware that Derek Green, one of Big Ed's top lieutenants, was in the club that night. He spotted Alvin and Vanessa all lovied up in the corner and called Big Ed on his cell phone, letting him know he'd found the two most wanted on Big Ed's list.

When Vanessa and Alvin left the club, they were greeted rudely by Donnie and Billy Ray. Alvin tried to put up a fight, which was a big mistake. The gruesome twosome beat him down savagely. Vanessa attempted to stop it and was promptly greeted by a thundering right cross to the jaw, courtesy of Billy Ray. Next they were duct-taped and unceremoniously slammed into the darkness of the Caddy's trunk.

The Hamilton Park Condos were nothing more than glorified apartments. Painted gray with royal blue trim, they appeared elegant. There was a huge swimming pool located directly in the center of the complex. It also housed an exercise/weight room, sauna, and social hall for tenant meetings and parties.

Vanessa unlocked the door and walked in. Big Ed followed. Flicking on the lights, she said, "Let me go get your money."

"I'll go with you," Big Ed stated, matter-of-factly.

"It's in the bedroom."

"My favorite place."

They went to the bedroom, where Vanessa opened the closet door and began reaching inside a shoe box. Big Ed, sensing danger, grabbed her wrist in a vice lock and with his free hand took the box from her. Letting her go, he opened the box and smiled at all the neatly stacked twenties, fifties, and hundred-dollar bills in it.

"I told you I won't cross you." She was rubbing her wrist.

"It's better safe than sorry," he said.

"Well, since it's like that, can I clean myself up?"

"Yeah baby, you look a mess."

Vanessa's next move caught Big Ed totally off guard. She stripped down to her burgundy-colored panties, picked up the tattered dress, and headed for the bathroom. Turning her head around at the door, she whispered, "Don't go anywhere."

Big Ed stood there with a dumbfounded look on his face, holding the box of bills. His hormones raged as he watched that fine piece of meat sashay down the hall. The fact that she left the door open while she brushed her teeth, washed her mouth out with Listerine, and combed her hair back before covering it with a shower cap only increased his desire.

"Baby, you know what you doin to me, don't you?" Big Ed was at the bathroom door.

"I haven't done anything yet." She faced him, giving him an up-close view of her stout frame.

"You keep that shit up and I'll be here all night."

"You're not staying?" She looked surprised.

"Hell yeah, I'm staying! Now take that shower and come to daddy!" Big Ed was all teeth.

Vanessa pirouetted on her heels, wiggled out of her underwear, bent over and reached for the faucets. Big Ed was drooling after receiving a lovely view of her pubic hairs. She also displayed a red rose tattoo on her right buttock. The left butt exhibited the Raiders pirate logo. His manhood now at full attention, Big Ed went into her living room, picked up the telephone, and dialed his cellular.

"Big Ed's." Flea was loaded.

"Flea, it's me."

"Yeah, Boss."

"Come up here for a minute and bring the phone with you."

"On my way."

When Flea got to the door, Big Ed was waiting. Handing over his keys, he told him, "Go to my crib and get my truck. Have Billy—naw, have Donnie follow you back here. Billy Ray ain't got no license. Leave the keys in the glove compartment and the door unlocked. I'll catch up with you tomorrow. If I need you, I'll beep you. Make sho you keep it turned on."

"A booty call, huh?" Flea was grinning.

"You know it, dawg—I'mo pop that cherry proper."

Flea strolled back to the Caddy as Big Ed closed the door. Returning to the living room, Ed sat down and peeped out Vanessa's crib. The sofa where he sat was green and white striped with a matching loveseat. Numerous matching pillows added a nice touch to this arrangement. White marbled coffee and end tables held coasters, magazines, candles, and candy dishes. Assorted plants placed everywhere gave Big Ed a feeling of being in the jungle.

An octagon-shaped tank with a variety of colorful fish sat to the left of a twenty-seven-inch floor-model television. On the right, she had a black component set. Above that to the right was a bird cage covered with a custom-made black sheet. In the corner was a tri-tiered photo display with pictures of Vanessa's family, along with many of her and Alvin.

Big Ed got up and placed every picture of Alvin face down. Alvin was history, and the sooner Vanessa accepted that fact, the better off she would be, or so Big Ed reasoned to himself. He wasn't coming home. Returning to his seat, he heard her turn off the shower so he grabbed the remote and turned on the TV.

Vanessa entered the room wearing a red silk negligee that barely covered her hips. Big Ed looked at her swollen jaw and felt sorry for her. The television was on Soulbeat, which is the only 100% black-owned and -operated station in the country. They were showing a music video. Plopping down on the sofa right next to him, she asked, "Would you like a drink or something to eat?"

"You need to put ice on yo face." He looked concerned.

"It's alright—at least I still have a face," she replied.

"You thought I was gonna kill you?" His question was sincere.

"Yes, I did," she answered truthfully.

"Baby, that thought never even crossed my mind."

"It didn't?" She was surprised.

"Why would I kill you when I think you would be the perfect woman for me?"

"Big Ed, you really don't know anything about me. You don't know my ways, my habits, my likes or dislikes...."

"I know I always wanted you."

"My body?" She wanted him to say what she'd always heard.

"Body, mind, heart, soul. See, baby, you ain't like us."

"Why do you say that?" She was curious.

"I say that 'cause you ain't even got to be in this environment. Yo daddy is a college professor, Momma's an elementary school teacher, you got a college degree."

"Those pieces of paper mean nothing to me."

"Maybe not, but I'll say this then I'mo leave it alone: You got style, class, come from the other side of the tracks, phine as fine can be, educated, cultured...."

"That doesn't mean a thing." She cut him off.

"That means you didn't need no fool like Alvin. I always wondered why you were with him—now I know." Big Ed was matter-of-fact with his conclusion.

"You know what?"

"I know those tattoos on yo ass represent rebellion."

"Rebel—"

"Rebellion to yo folks. They've probably been over-pro-tective since you was a little girl. I'd be willin ta bet they didn't like Al, won't like me, and you couldn't give a damn. It probably makes you happy knowin you make them miserable. See, that pirate on yo ass is something you done 'cause you know they'd have a heart attack if they ever saw it. But let me ask, why would a pretty woman like you have the Raiders on yo butt?"

"I'm a football fan and the Raiders are my team."

"They my team too, but I ain't gone tattoo my ass to prove it."

"You don't understand. Since I was little my daddy always had season tickets to the Raiders. Even when they moved to L.A., we would still catch a plane down there for their home games. That was always our time together, Football Sunday."

"Oh, so what you sayin is since the Raiders are eight and two, and they play Dallas Sunday, you gone be at the game?" he asked.

"Yes, that's what I'm saying."

"Wit yo daddy?"

"No, daddy doesn't go anymore. He says the team is Hollywoodized, but I know he hated the Marcus Allen fiasco."

"So yaw don't go to the games no mo."

"No more," she corrected his pronunciation. "I raffle off my two tickets at work every week, usually making a hundred and fifty dollars, but for the Cowboys or Niners, I wouldn't miss it for the world."

"So why didn't you take Alvin?"

"He always said I acted stupid and embarrassed him."

"How?"

"Because I'm a die-hard. I know more about football than most men I've been with and they can't handle it. Would you like to go to the game Sunday?"

"You got tickets to the GAME?" He was excited.

"Yes, I do. If you'd like, I'll stop raffling them off and we can go to every home game together."

Without another word Vanessa rose to her feet, headed for the kitchen, and began fixing them both some drinks. After handing Big Ed his shot, setting a coaster in front of him then placing hers on one, she headed for the bedroom. Turning around at the door she whispered, "Don't go anywhere."

Big Ed still wasn't convinced. Upon her return from the room, he told her, "You take a drink from my glass."

Vanessa handed him the tickets to the Raiders/Dallas game then gulped down half of his drink. Before handing her glass to him she drank some of that one, then headed for the kitchen to refill what used to be his drink. Returning, she plopped down on the sofa, sighed, then spoke: "What will it take to prove to you that I won't cross you?"

"A whole lot," he said then gulped down some of his drink. "What is this?" he asked while looking curiously at his glass.

"It's called a mimosa," she responded.

"A memowhat?"

"Mimosa—that's orange juice and champagne."

"Hell, I thought it was gin and juice." He drank some more.

"Do you like it?"

"It tastes OK."

"Let me fix you another one."

As she reached over to retrieve his glass, he pulled her into his arms and softly kissed her lips. Caressing her thighs and hip, he let her go. Vanessa was surprised by how gentle Big Ed was with her. Alvin and many of her previous lovers were rough, too anxious, and didn't understand foreplay. Just the fact that he hadn't mauled her yet left her curious. After she refilled their shots, he resumed his rap.

"See, that's what I'm talking about."

"What?" she inquired.

"Most women I know think champagne is for special occasions, but you drink it with juice whenever you feel like it."

"It's almost five—wouldn't you like to get comfortable?"

"Who said I wasn't comfortable?" he shot back.

Vanessa was getting miffed. Most men would not hesitate when she offered her wares, but Big Ed didn't seem that enthused by her proposition. Not only did this surprise her, it piqued her curiosity.

"Baby, I'm offering my body to you," she told him directly.

"I can get booty all over town, Ness."

"Not this one."

"What makes yours any different?" It was more a statement than a question. He continued, "See, all them fools you been fuckin wit went 'Coo-Coo fa Cocoa Puffs' just because dey was gone get in yo draws. I ain't like that— I want to understand yo mental makeup. I can get pussy anytime I want it. Shit, I could go down to San Pablo Avenue and buy the shit with no strings attached. Yo body is lovely, I'll give you yo propahs on that, but that's not what I'm about."

"Well, what ARE you about, honey?" She was syrupy.

"I'm about dead presidents."

"'Dead presidents'?"

"Money," he stated boldly.

"Money isn't everything," she returned.

"But it will get you everything, making life a joy. See, Ness, I like to live in luxury, and without money that just won't happen. When people say shit like you just said, I know they talkin out the side of they neck. For example, if I was a broke muthafucka you wouldn't give me the time of day. But since you know my bank stays fat and I keep money in all foe pockets, far as you concerned I'm cool. So money does mean something."

Vanessa was speechless, because no other man spoke the truth to her the way Big Ed did. She finished off her drink then rose to pour another when Big Ed stood, scooped her in his arms effortlessly, and headed for the bedroom. Pausing briefly, he kissed her more softly than the first time. Her tongue was eagerly meeting his, and since she had never been kissed while off her feet, her desire increased.

Laying her down lightly on the bed, Big Ed took off his turtleneck and folded it neatly. Next, he slipped out of his shoes, socks, then his Levis, taking particular care to neatly arrange each item. Her eyes now adjusted, she saw his muscular frame silhouetted in the dark. She slid out of her negligee and got under the covers.

Big Ed joined her in bed, then lay on his back with his arm around her neck staring at the ceiling in silence. Vanessa cuddled up to him and began running her hands up and down his rock-solid frame. As her hand snaked towards his penis, he brushed it aside then with his hands he spread her legs apart.

While he softly kissed her nipples, his thick fingers massaged her clit. As Vanessa stirred Big Ed worked his lips all over her torso. He was treating her body as delicately as fine china, which had Vanessa's love box turning into a raging inferno.

Once his thick finger began plunging in and out of her hole, her body responded in rhythm. Feeling his phat pole on her leg, she tried to angle her thrusts just right so he could enter, but Big Ed would have none of that.

He took his sweet time exploring every inch of her body while she wiggled and humped non-stop. Satisfied with his work, Big Ed raised his body above hers and whispered, "You ready for this?"

"Yes," she responded huskily.

Before the word exited her tongue, Big Ed penetrated. Moving in slow rhythmic motions he inched his way deep inside of her. Vanessa had never been so full. Just when she thought he was at his full length, he would go deeper. Her plan was to whoop and holler, moan, groan, and make him think he was whipping it on her, but it backfired.

Big Ed was stretching her like never before, and when Vanessa did begin moaning, it was for real. She attempted to speed up the action but Big Ed was slow and deliberate with his strokes. Vanessa felt Big Ed hitting spots that had never been explored, and when she orgasmed it seemed to make his manhood that much larger.

He paused for a second and she thought he would unload. Bracing for his juice, she was surprised when he grabbed the top edges of the mattress and turned into a human battering ram. Vanessa's legs became jelly and she began mumbling incoherently. All the while Big Ed stroked her with a force she'd never known. He lifted up her right leg and plunged so far into her body that she screamed out in pleasure. She was in love, but he still wasn't finished.

Cupping both of her ass cheeks with his beefy hands, he plowed into her with reckless abandon. Vanessa thrashed her head from side to side, kissed his chest, arms, shoulders—anywhere her lips would reach—accepting his full force with every ounce of passion in her body.

For the first time in her life, Vanessa Harris was sexually whipped. Big Ed continued to dick her down for the next twenty minutes, which to Ness seemed like hours. She loved every minute of it. Alvin couldn't hold a candle to what she was now getting. Although she felt like collapsing from exhaustion, she knew she had to continue letting him have his way, and have his way he did.

Right when she felt her love box getting dry Big Ed barked, "Turn over."

Vanessa rolled onto her stomach. Big Ed pulled her up to her knees then penetrated doggy style. Although she was stuffed like a bell pepper, the backdoor sex instantly lubricated her again. Her fingers reached for air while Big Ed controlled her hips and plowed viciously into her. Letting off his load, Big Ed rose up and headed for the bathroom. Pausing at the door, he asked, "How was it, Ness?"

"Baby, that's the best I've ever had." She spoke the truth.

Big Ed knew it, but he wanted to hear it from the horse's mouth. Grinning, he went to take a shower. When he returned to the room, Vanessa was dreamily gazing at him.

"So where do we go from here?" she asked.

"Where do you want to go?" he asked back.

"I don't know because I really don't know what you have in mind for me."

"Ness, look, it's like this. You know I have a wife."

"Yes, I know Shirley," she said dryly.

"Then you know she's the mother of my kids, right?"

"Yes."

"Well, baby, I'mo be truthful with you. I can't walk away from my kids but I would love to have you in my corner. I need a woman like you because like I said earlier, you got class."

"So basically what you're saying is you want me as your mistress?" She was matter-of-fact.

"No, what I'm saying is I want you as my woman. You may not know it, but me and Shirley's relationship has been fucked up for years."

"Then why do you stay with her?"

"She has my kids and if I leave, she'll use them as a

weapon against me. She plays Miss Goody Two-Shoes, but what people don't know is that she's an evil bitch."

"I still don't see how I fit in—I really don't like love triangles."

Vanessa sat propped with her head resting on her hands. Big Ed lay down next to her on his back. The minute he did, Vanessa's free hand involuntarily rubbed his chest.

"It ain't no triangle, Ness—you just have to be patient."

Vanessa wanted to be difficult and say something sarcastic, which was her nature, but she thought the better of it and kept quiet. After realizing that she was in a no-win situation and didn't want to lose the one man who took her over the edge, she spoke timidly: "OK, I'll do whatever it takes to have you as my man."

That said, Ed got on top of her and resumed taking her heart with his lovemaking. After he was done, he rolled over on his back to catch his breath. When he looked at Ness, she was out like a light. She was the first woman he'd ever known who didn't get "sore" and have to stop before he got his rocks off. Big Ed had a foot-long dick that would hurt most women because he was not a true cocksman. He would just bang the shit out of them, thinking all their screams were of pleasure, when in fact he would be causing nothing but pain. Speaking to himself he said, "Baby, you're the one." He slept peacefully that day.

Vanessa woke up before Big Ed and headed for the restroom. Her vagina was sore and felt as if Ed's beef were still in it. Sitting on the toilet she began to urinate. Normally she could control her flow but today it just streamed out.

The sensations flowing through her body caused her

mind to dream. Remembering how wonderful Big Ed made her feel, she smiled. Wiping off the drip, she flushed the toilet then took a shower.

Stopping at the bedroom door, she gazed at him sleeping peacefully, then put on a negligee and walked painfully to the kitchen. He'd put a hurt on her and she knew it. It was a good hurt, though—the kind of hurt she would now crave daily.

Big Ed rolled over and inhaled the fumes waffling through the air. Thinking about the wonderful sex with Vanessa, he knew it was only the beginning of what would be a beautiful relationship. Glancing at the clock, he saw that it displayed four P.M.

Picking up the remote, he turned on her television. It was on the news channel and they were showing the murder scene. The anchorman was describing how the body found was unidentifiable due to the savagery of the killing. He went on to say that sources who wished to remain "anonymous" claimed it to be a drug murder, thus justifying the execution style in which it was carried out. Next, they showed the task force raiding houses and arresting street-corner dealers.

Usually, he would be upset by the drug sweep, but today he was not. This would give him a few days with Vanessa without business interrupting him. It also provided a built-in excuse with Shirley because he could just say that he was caught in the dragnet and went to jail.

Big Ed put on his underwear and wandered into the kitchen. The smell of bacon frying made him realize just how famished he was.

"Smells good," he commented as he sat.

"Good afternoon, baby—breakfast will be ready in a minute." She kissed him then continued preparing his meal.

"How did you sleep?" He knew the answer.

"I slept like a baby," she smiled.

"What's on your schedule for today?"

"I don't have any plans. I called my job and told them I wasn't feeling well, which really means I'm free for you. Do you like your eggs with cheese?"

"Yes I do."

She sat his plate on the table then fixed herself one with smaller portions. The menu was bacon, cheese eggs scrambled, hash browns, and biscuits. While pouring his juice she asked him, "Did you say your blessing?"

"No, I don't do that."

Joining him at the table, she said, "Give me your hands." Holding hands she began, "Lord, thank you for the food we are about to receive and bless us with the nourishment it will provide. In Jesus' name we pray. Amen."

"Amen," Big Ed mumbled with a mouth full of food.

"Is the food satisfactory?" she asked a few moments later.

"This shit on hits, baby."

"You call my food shit?"

"It's just an expression—that's the way I talk, nothing personal."

"What do you have planned today?"

"I don't know yet. It depends on how much damage the police have done."

"Damage the police have done?" She didn't understand.

"I just saw on the news where the task force was on another one of their raids. So every time they do that, they put us out of business for a few days."

"What do you usually do when this happens?"

"I get ghost, take my kids to some amusement park or Disneyland. By the time I get back the heat is off."

Vanessa was amazed at how quickly Big Ed ate his food. Taking his plate, she served him up everything remaining on the stove and watched in awe as he wolfed it down. His cell phone rang but before he could get up Vanessa handed it to him.

"Talk to me," he spoke.

"Boss, it's me," Flea shouted.

"Whatup, dawg?"

"They raided yo house. Don't go home."

"What about Shirley and my boys?"

"Since they didn't find shit, they let them go. They only wanted you."

"OK, here's what you do, Flea. Don't tell Shirley shit unless she asks—matter of fact, try to avoid her. Then if she catches up with you, get amnesia."

"OK, Boss, I'ont know nuthin."

"Good! Where Billy and Don at?"

"They right here with me, Boss."

"OK, tell those fools to lay low for the next few days and stay out of mischief."

"You got it."

"Awight Flea, I'll call you in a few days. I'm gettin ghost."

"OK, Boss, have fun."

"Check." Big Ed hung up.

"Pack your bags," Big Ed ordered Vanessa.

She rose from the table, scooping up the plates in one motion, then washed the dishes and headed for the bedroom. Big Ed went to the room, got dressed, then told Vanessa, "I'll be right back."

He walked out the door and was back in three minutes carrying an oversized athletic bag. Pulling out several neatly folded garments, he handed her a pair of black slacks, a black silk shirt, and a portable iron.

"Take care of this while I shower."

He stripped down naked as Vanessa gazed loving at the baseball bat hanging between his legs. It looked like a monster. She was busy ironing before he got to the bathroom. When he returned to the room, he reached inside his bag and pulled out underwear, socks, hair grease, lotion, a toothbrush, and cologne.

Splashing on Aramis, he put on his briefs took the toothbrush and strode back into the bathroom. After Big Ed completed his methodical dressing ritual, which lasted longer than any man Vanessa had ever known, he picked up the luggage and they walked out the front door.

"Let's take yo ride," he said.

They hopped in her car with Big Ed sliding into the driver's side. It was an Acura Legend coupe, candy-apple red and very clean. Big Ed pulled the seat lever and slid all the way back for the leg room he needed, then started up the engine and rolled.

4
FIVE-O ROUND-UP

The Oaktown Police Department was bustling with activity as usual. Prostitutes, spousal abusers, drunk drivers, and various other criminals were being hauled in and shuffled around the precinct office. After the booking process, which consisted of a strip-down search, being fingerprinted, having money and personal items taken to the property unit, and giving a written statement of their side of the facts (recorded by officers on duty), those arrested were led to the holding cells.

There many would find a spot on the floor or bench, use the collect-calls-only telephone, or sit silently wondering how they got themselves into the current predicament. Others, usually regulars, would talk nonstop to anyone willing to hold a conversation. When they could find no takers, they would talk out loud to themselves.

The stories were always familiar: "The police were

wrong," "I was just minding my own business," "If I was white I would have been treated differently," "I got a lawyer and we gonna sue the city...." Gnats flew around as if they owned the place, the phone stayed occupied, musk filled your nostrils from the moment you entered, and you did eventually lose track of time.

Unknown to the prisoners or public, a gang of officers was assembling in back of the station. This unit consisted of vice, SWAT, the gang unit, and uniformed personnel. They would be assisted by members of the Drug Enforcement Agency (DEA), Alcohol-Tobacco and Firearms (ATF), Sergeants, Captains, Lieutenants, and a Deputy Chief.

Their mission: Sweep the streets clean of all drug dealers. It didn't matter what level pusher they were, only that they would be temporarily out of business. The police had to show the media and the public that they were in control of the city's volatile drug situation.

Armed with battering rams, rapid-fire weapons, bullet-proof vests, search warrants, and the knowledge that they held the element of surprise, they loaded up in paddy wagons and squad cars. Wherever they went that day, they would outnumber the criminals at least ten to one. Considering it was seven in the morning, most targets would be asleep, unprepared, and surprised. Five-O had the edge and knew it.

The procedure was planned and had been done on many occasions. Parking down the street from the occupant's home, they would surround the place entirely. Communication was by radio transmitters clipped on their collars, along with earplugs.

Once in position, they would knock/pound on the door and yell, "Police, open up!" Before anyone had time to move, the officers would break down the front and back doors using battering rams, then bum-rush the home.

Simultaneously, windows would be smashed, curtains yanked to the floor, and guns trained on anything moving. The noise generated sounded like an earthquake and would wake up the entire block. As people groggily looked out their doors or windows, what they saw was Five-O hauling out every member of the household along with safes, drugs, guns, and anything else that could be used against them in court.

By the time their mission was complete, the house would resemble a shack. Some neighbors were happy that their block was finally rid of a bad element, while others re-affirmed their belief that OPD didn't care one bit about people's personal possessions.

Several of the homes were owned by parents or grandparents who had little or no knowledge of the activities of their offspring. The fact that their home was ransacked and the occupants treated as common criminals left a sour taste in their mouths that would be with them for the rest of their lives.

The media tagged along with reporters and cameramen, interviewing neighbors, snapping photos, and videotaping everything. Meanwhile, the police were backslapping each other while tooting their own horn to the press. They would talk about "the danger involved" in what they were doing, how they were "glad to work with a group of dedicated staff," and "the streets would be safer now. . . ."

45

Hitting every "hotspot" on its list, which covered all parts of town, the task force accomplished what it set out to do. Drug users would have a difficult time finding dope, but after regrouping, dealers would usually be back at it within a few days.

As the task force was zeroing in on drug houses, the narc squad and uniformed patrol officers were hitting every known "problem" street corner in the city. They would roll up five cars deep on a corner or park, and as the low-level dealers "got ghost," the foot chases began.

Many of the street hoods were fat, out of shape, or unable to escape because their baggy pants hanging down wouldn't allow them to hit full stride. In several chases the scene presented to passing motorists was hilarious. The rollers would be in hot pursuit, holding their billy clubs, with the thugs running and steadily pulling up their pants. Five-O had practice running this way, the hoods did not.

Once caught, some made the mistake of trying to resist. But the officers were highly trained in hand-to-hand combat. Going through their twenty-six-week training course, they were presented with every imaginable situation. Many cadets would get their arms broken or limbs sprained just from training, so once they hit the streets they were prepared.

The end result would be officers bringing back their prisoners looking fresh, while the soon-to-be-incarcerated looked tired, out of breath, and beat up. For one day at least, the streets were clean. You could walk into your favorite store without the usual mob scene outside the door.

Back at headquarters, the homicide unit was working overtime to solve murders. Even the open-and-shut cases were hard to prove because witnesses would not talk for fear of retaliation. Murders were happening at an alarming rate due to the drug wars. With the sweep going on, homicide detectives knew the killing spree would slow down. They also knew the emphasis would be on them to assist the DA's office with successful prosecution of suspected murderers.

Detectives Johnson and Hernandez reported for their swing shift assignment and were immediately met at the door of their second-floor office by deputy chief Spitz. He was in a lousy mood, which was his daily disposition.

"You two, in my office!" he snapped.

Johnson and Hernandez followed Spitz into his small, cramped office and sat down. Spitz grabbed a stack of file folders on his desk, then slammed them back down.

"Goddammit, I want closure. These fucking files have been lying around for weeks without any of the murders solved, yet you ACE detectives continue to receive paychecks." His words were heavily laced with sarcasm.

"Sir, we are doing all we can. Without cooperation from witnesses, these cases are almost impossible to prove on evidence alone. You know that." Johnson spoke slowly in measured tones. Hernandez sat stone-faced.

"All I know, JOHNSON, is that the chief plus the damn DA's office are on my ass for results, and you two provide me with diddly-squat."

"Sir, we've covered all our bases, and in time, people will step forward," Johnson said.

"Well, that may be true but we need convictions NOW!" Spitz screamed. After a brief pause he continued, "Look, gentlemen, this just came in. A body was found by someone jogging near Lookout Point. The victim's hands were severed at the wrists and his face was blown to smithereens. Here's the location." Spitz handed Johnson a stickum memo and resumed his rap. "See if we can solve this one, OK?"

"Yes, sir," they both said in unison as they headed for their desks.

Spitz walked out, heading for the basement cafeteria while Johnson and Hernandez watched with disgust. They hated this little man. Adam Spitz III was a racist and everybody knew it. His promotions were due to outright lobbying from his father and uncle, who both were retired cops.

Standing five foot seven and weighing one forty, Spitz resembled a bookworm—someone you were more likely to see working in a library than a police station. He wore bi-focals and outdated suits, which only increased his nerdy appearance.

As racist as they came, Spitz felt that he was superior to blacks, Latinos, and Asians and hated the fact that affirmative-action programs allowed them to "contaminate" the force. His people skills were poor due to the fact that he grew up in a lily-white environment and had no understanding of minority cultures.

Nathan Johnson was a proud black man. At six foot six, three hundred pounds, he was huge. A product of the ghetto, he originally joined the force to help his people. In time, he realized that some of them couldn't be helped, so he concentrated on the ones who could. He gave up much of his free time doing community service work, coaching youth sports programs, speaking at his alma mater, and assisting with recruitment drives.

Nathan was of the mind that he could make a difference in his community. The fact that he no longer resided in "his community" was insignificant. He believed that since he was born and raised there, that could never be taken away, and he would always hold a special place in his heart for Oaktown—the west side in particular.

Manuel Hernandez was a different story. He stood a meager five foot nine, one hundred and eighty pounds, which was rapidly turning to flab. Manny tried to openly distance himself from his Latino heritage. After he married a white woman who bore his half-breed children, then started talking and acting white, his compadres were furious.

The Mexican community held dances, proclamations, and Manuel Hernandez Days to acknowledge his rapid rise in his profession. After giving him so much credit for being an asset to his race, the mere mention of his name in barrios brought looks of disgust to most faces. Stung by the criticism, Hernandez would rough up Latinos twice as viciously as any other nationality when arresting them. He didn't really care for blacks, which caused many tense moments between him and Nate, but for some unexplained reason, he treated his own worse.

Looking at the memo, Nate spoke to his partner.

"Manny, let's get the service vehicle and take a drive to the Point."

"Where a million clues wait for us, right, Nathan?"
They both smiled.

"Look, we'll just see what we have to go on and take
it from there."

"OK, partner," Manny said.

They headed for the door, only to be met by Sargeant
Evans. Hernandez greeted him first.

"Johnnie my man, how ya doin?"

"I'm fine, sir. Mister Johnson—" Nate nodded his head.

"What brings you here, amigo?"

"I need to talk to you guys. We have a suspect in custody for a 212 who says he knows about one of your cases."

"Which case?" Johnson boomed.

"The Turner case, sir," Evans responded.

"What does he know?"

"He claims he knows who did it."

"Good work, Evans—we'll question him when we get
back. It goes without saying that he wants immunity from
prosecution, right?" Johnson stated matter-of-factly.

"That's right, sir, but I told him I couldn't promise anything."

"Good. What's the prisoner's name?" Johnson asked.

"Roscoe Porter."

As Evans said the name, Manny jotted it down.

Johnson spoke again: "We'll question Porter when we
return. Let's go, Manny."

They headed out the door and walked across the street
to transportation. Once there, Hernandez went to get their
service vehicle while Johnson signed out for it. After filling it with fuel, they headed for Lookout Point.

The murder scene at the Point was just like all the rest—reporters and media personnel trying to gather enough information for a story, citizens curiously gawking, uniformed officers roping off sections and questioning the joggers who stumbled upon the corpse, crime lab technicians snapping photos, crime scene investigators looking for clues, and employees from the coroner's office patiently waiting to haul the body away.

Johnson got out first and was swarmed by the media.

"Detective Johnson, what can you tell us?" asked one.

"I just arrived."

"Do you think it was a drug killing?" shot another.

"I don't know."

"Are there any witnesses?"

Johnson waved them off, stating, "Ladies and gentlemen, we will give you a full report once all pertinent information becomes available to us. Then and only then can I make an official statement. Now, if you'll excuse me, I have a job to do."

Bulling his way through the crowd, Johnson headed over to the very dead body surrounded by uniformed officers. Looking it over for anything that could be of help in identifying it, he noticed a tattoo. "Get me an up-close shot of this," he told one of the crime lab techs. "Somebody cover it up!" His voice boomed.

One of the officers headed for his patrol unit to retrieve a blanket but the coroner's assistant beat him to the punch with a body bag. Hernandez strolled up to Johnson with a disgusted look on his face.

"What's up?" Johnson asked his partner.

"Absolutely zilch." Manny was dejected.

"I guess that means we have to wait for the victim to be identified."

"It's worse than that, Nate."

"How so?"

"Whoever committed this crime knew exactly what they were doing. They blew off the victim's face and chopped off his hands, so identification is virtually impossible. I can just hear Spitz threatening my job already." Manny was animated.

"Let's go to the station and question Porter."

Johnson gave his partner the Polaroid snapshot of the tattoo. Hernandez read the wording aloud.

"Al & Ness—2gether 4ever. How cute." His voice dripped with sarcasm.

"More than likely the dude's name is Al or some variation of that, but Manny, I believe that if we find 'Ness,' we solve the murder."

"Good logic, partner."

They got in their service vehicle and headed back downtown to headquarters. Parking on Seventh Street in a spot "reserved for police use only," they entered through the front plate-glass doors and took the stairs to the second floor, which housed the criminal investigations division. This consisted of mostly desk sargeants whose job consisted of doing follow-up investigations on every written report by patrol officers from the day and night before.

The desk sargeants were assigned different areas of the city to carry out follow-up investigations of any crime committed on their beat. Many departments across the country had "specialists" who handled one particular type of crime. So if you specialized in strong-armed robbery, for example, you would get those cases.

By being assigned whatever happened in their jurisdiction, several officers felt as if their talent was not being used correctly. They also felt like they were the laughingstock of police work nationwide. Management thought differently, feeling that if you were exceptional at solving carjackings but couldn't solve a domestic violence case, you were in the wrong profession.

There were hundreds of reports made daily, and like most divisions, not enough manpower. This fact was not lost on employees. Job burnout occurred easily, along with angering certain employees every day because they felt their talents were being wasted.

At least six interrogation rooms were located on this floor. They were all small—eight by ten—and consisted of a table, two or three chairs, and a two-way peephole. Each door had a slot provided for the inmate's paperwork.

The arresting officers wrote in what time the prisoner entered the room, then logged in every action. Whoever went in the room, for whatever reason, had to write it down. So the sheet would have what time they brought the person a meal, let them use the restroom, looked in, or interviewed them.

These rooms were generally occupied between the hours of one to seven A.M., and housed only people who'd committed serious or violent crimes. Eyewitnesses would also be placed in these rooms, but for them, the door would remain open with an officer sitting guard right outside of it.

Johnson and Hernandez walked up to the interrogation room door, looked at the prisoner sheet, then unlocked the door and opened it. The room was empty. The acoustic ceiling was laid on the floor and the chair remained on top of the table.

"Damn, the dirty bastard escaped!" Hernandez stated with disgust.

"The sheet says he's only thirty minutes ahead of us. Manny, that means he probably is still in the building. Call for the dogs."

Manny radioed for a police dog while simultaneously, Roscoe Porter dropped down from the ceiling in front of the homicide door and exited the building on Washington Street. He had crawled the length of the building, stopping occasionally to slightly lift a ceiling square and see if the coast was clear.

Casually walking across the street, he saw the officers running into the station with two dogs. Knowing they were after him, Porter joined the throng of homeless people sleeping in front of the county courthouses. Helping himself to a filthy blanket left in a shopping cart, he spread it out amongst the poor, covered up, and waited.

Hernandez returned with the dogs and let them loose in the air ducts. He and Johnson followed their barks through the office until they exited criminal investigations and saw ceiling tile on the floor in front of homicide. The dogs jumped out dumbfounded, with Hernandez spewing obscenities.

"Punk-ass motherfucker escaped! I'll be damned."

"Calm down, Manny, we'll get him."

"Asshole probably wasn't gonna talk anyway. I hate it when it gets dark at five o'clock."

With summer over, daylight savings time ended with it. Fall represented darkness hitting at five. This gave Roscoe Porter a head start because the homeless set up camp as soon as county offices close.

Porter was a repeat offender, so he knew he would be facing California's "three strikes, you're out" law. That meant a possible life sentence, which he was determined not to serve. If he could not work a deal telling on somebody, he'd try to escape.

Porter was a product of the ghetto. Six four, two fifty, he was big and bad. He knew that snitching on Slack was dangerous, but if it came down to Slack or his ass, his own came in first every time.

He had seen Slack enter the DeFermery Park bathroom on the Fourth of July but never saw him leave. The next day when he read about the murder of Eddie Turner, a small-time hustler, in that same bathroom, he knew that Slack did it. And if he had to sell Slack's ass to save his own? Oh well.

Johnson put out an all-points bulletin on Porter, then they decided to try and get a lead on the corpse's tattoo. Hernandez headed for the third-floor fingerprint office where he poured through photos, while Johnson ran a description into his computer. One hour later, Hernandez struck pay dirt.

"Nate, I got a match. The victim is one Alvin Duane Jenkins, street hustler. Lives on Golf Links with his woman Vanessa Harris."

"Good shit, Manny—let's go question the girl."

Exiting the station, they rolled to the east side, where they hoped to get answers from Vanessa. Since they didn't know what she looked like, they never saw her as she and Big Ed drove right past them.

Realizing that no one was home at the condominium, Johnson stuck his card into the security door and they walked back to their ride.

"You wanna wait?" asked Hernandez.

"No, Manny—we'll find her soon enough."

"Where to now, partner?"

"Let's grab a bite to eat."

"Good call, Nate."

They drove back downtown and parked in front of Mexicali Rose, the preferred spot for their nightly dinner break. On occasion they would eat elsewhere for a change of pace, but Mexicali Rose was number one on their list. Located one block from headquarters, the restaurant was painted pink, with a green neon sign proudly displaying its name. The interior was always dimly lit, providing exquisite ambiance for patrons. The food was good, prices reasonable, and the atmosphere excellent.

They ate in silence, each man absorbed in his own thoughts. Johnson ordered a super steak burrito à la carte; Hernandez chose a beef and cheese quesadilla. He always placed his order in Spanish but it never impressed the staff.

Meanwhile, Roscoe Porter rose up, flipped off the blanket, and blended in with the crowd. Walking swiftly down Broadway, he got on the number 88 bus going to the west side.

He lived on 10th and Center with his wife Wilma but chose not to go there. He knew the Man would be waiting. Instead he went to his girlfriend Sonya's house.

Sonya Haynes had been in love with Roscoe for ten years. She knew he'd never leave Wilma and didn't really care. Four kids by three different men, a life spent on government aid, low self-esteem, and a bleak future, she was satisfied just knowing that he would rock her world a couple of times a week.

A country girl, Sonya was high yellow with big breasts, big mouth, large ass, and a thick body. She lived on 18th and Linden in a Section 8 rented house. Roscoe would come around whenever he felt like it and mow her lawn along with doing patchwork and minor repairs to the place. Once he was finished, she'd close her bedroom door, slide the dresser drawer up against it, and let him have his pleasure. He'd hit it so hard that her vagina would make farting noises, causing her to say "excuse me."

Roscoe walked through the door and was instantly angry. Sonya was sitting on the sofa with another man, so close that their legs were touching.

"Hey baby," she said.

"Let me talk to you." He headed for the kitchen.

"Roscoe, this is my friend Elliot. El, dis mah man Roscoe."

Elliot rose to shake Roscoe's hand but he would have none of that.

"Sit down, niggah, dis don't concern you. You, in here!" He jerked his thumb towards the kitchen.

"I'll be right back," Sonya told Elliot.

They entered the kitchen and Roscoe began.

SHAKEY'S LOOSE

"Girl, ain't ah done tole you 'bout havin niggahs in heah?"

"Baby, he's an old friend, almost like a brother."

"Brother mah ass! I seen da body language."

"Roscoe!" she screamed.

"Fuck dat shit, tell da niggah ta leave."

"Roscoe, I ain't gone do that! You need ta quit trippin."

"Oh, now ahm trippin?"

"You always trip anytime you see me wit another man, yet I don't say shit when you go home to your WIFE!" She was just as loud as he was.

He grabbed her by the throat roughly, then whispered, "You bettah tell dat niggah ta leave or ahm'o kick his ass and yo's too."

Elliot couldn't help but overhear the entire conversation, and upon hearing Roscoe's threats of violence, he cut out. By the time Sonya came back from the kitchen, he was long gone, never to return.

"I ain't got ta tell him shit 'cause he gone," she stated angrily.

"Why you so mad?" Roscoe was pleased.

"You didn't have ta go there."

"I go wherever da fuck ah wanna go, bitch."

"Fuck you, you sorry excuse for a man."

Before the words left her mouth, he fired. The force of the blow knocked her down.

"Bitch, who you callin sorry? I'll whup yo punk ass. You thank since you been goin ta dat welfare-ta-work class, you all lat. You still ain't shit, and as long as ah live and breathe, you mah bitch, you understand?"

"Yes, I understand." she spoke timidly.

"What you got ta drank?"

"I didn't get to the store yet."

"Well, just give me some money so I can go buy me some beer."

She reached for her purse while feeling her lip for blood. Handing over a twenty-dollar bill, Sonya felt sorry for herself. She knew what Roscoe had done was wrong, but she just didn't have the courage to stand up to him.

He snatched the scrill out of her hand then bounced. Sonya's home was situated in the middle of the block, so Roscoe headed down the street for the corner store. Just as he reached 18th, he peeped Five-O but it was too late— the officer spotted him first.

Flicking the switch on his siren, the cop accelerated to the curb and hopped out with his gun drawn. The engine remained running as the tail end of the squad car blocked an entire lane.

"Freeze, you're under arrest!" the officer shouted as he took dead aim.

"Man, what you doin? Ah ain't did shit!"

The policeman was a young black guy named Jamison who'd been on the force for a year. He was five foot eleven, one eighty, but appeared smaller. He radioed for backup. By now a crowd had assembled.

"Put your hands behind your head, lock your fingers together, then drop to your knees!" he shouted with authority.

"Man, ah tole you ah ain't did nothing."

Roscoe did as instructed then Jamison moved up behind

him and placed a cuff on his right wrist, reciting his Miranda rights. Returning his gun to the holster, he started to cuff the left wrist when Roscoe sprang to his feet, turned around, and body-slammed him.

Jamison's head bounced off the pavement three times, leaving him punch drunk. Roscoe began kicking him while Jamison tried to grab his leg. Dropping to his knees, Roscoe pummeled his face into a bloody mess while citizens stood by doing nothing.

Jamison pulled his revolver and fired. The shot knocked Roscoe on his back. He was dead instantly. As children ran off crying to tell their parents what they'd just witnessed, the block was swarmed by cops.

By the time Johnson and Hernandez arrived on the scene, chaos reigned. Sonya came running down the street and upon seeing Roscoe's dead corpse, accused the police of excessive force. She was hysterical, blabbering loud and long about police brutality.

"Yaw ain't had ta kill mah man!" she screamed while crying over Roscoe's body.

"Ma'am, you'll have to step back," Johnson said softly.

"Aw fuck you, yaw done killed mah man!"

"Ma'am, if you don't get up, we'll have to arrest you."

"Arrest me then, muthafucka! You done kilt mah god-damn man, ain't shit else you can do ta me dat's gone hurt."

Johnson slowly lifted Sonya to her feet while the trou-blemakers in the crowd stirred the pot.

"See, da po po ain't shit without a gun and a mutha-fuckin badge!" someone hollered.

60

"Yeah!" the crowd retorted.

"He ain't had ta shoot 'im," someone else said.

"Know das right!" shouted another.

Sonya ran over to the paramedics who were busy placing Jamison on a gurney and screamed, "Why you kill mah man? You didn't hafta do that, you muthafucka! Ah hope yo ass rot in hell, you bastahd!"

Jamison's eyes were swollen shut, blood poured from his mouth, and he saw three of her. Even so, Sonya's words stung. He'd never killed anyone, so the entire series of events was very traumatic to him.

She didn't seem to notice that he was beat down, only that Roscoe was dead. She continued to scream profanities at the police until she noticed a van pull up and Wilma get out. Sonya knew what Wilma looked like, but Wilma didn't know her.

Wilma Porter was straight 5150, which is a police expression for crazy. Her skin was dark brown and rough as leather. She had big bug eyes, puffed-out jaws, a missing front tooth, rashy ears, and a gold-flowered scarf on her head, which was rolled up into a knot on her forehead.

She wore a dirty white negligee that displayed her huge sagging titties along with mushroom-sized nipples. It was tucked into black wrinkled jeans that were filled out by her huge ass. The tennis shoes she wore were very cheap and could be purchased from any five-and-dime store for two dollars.

Wilma came ready to rumble and didn't care who her foe would be—all she was certain of was the fact that her husband would not be coming home again. Slowly but surely, Sonya faded into the crowd, then imitated Houdini and disappeared.

Wilma took her place grieving her man while hearing one-sided versions of the story from onlookers. Hernandez noticed and shook his head.

"Nate, it looks like he had two women."

"Yes Manny, that appears to be true."

The media arrived. Newspaper and television reporters gathered facts while cameramen zoomed in on Roscoe's prone figure. They also showed the ambulance driving away with Jamison in it, lights and sirens blaring.

As word spread through the hood, the crowd swelled, with many agitators trying to instigate a riot. The police were ready, with at least seventy-five officers, many in riot gear, determined to control the mob.

Johnson's transmitter announced a drive-by shooting on 63rd and Aileen, the north side. Knowing that the present case was open and shut, he summoned Hernandez. Together they hopped in the Crown Victoria and sped towards that location.

The dispatch operator informed them that the shooting was a possible homicide. There were no casualties yet, but the gunplay was definitely drug-related. Pulling up on the block, the two detectives got out and began their normal routine of trying to gather facts.

BACK ON
THE BLOCK

Nadine pulled the Camaro into her driveway then killed the engine. Shakey sat there in a trance, his mind a million miles away. The drive home was quick even though they ran into the usual traffic from Powell Street to the MacArthur Maze. It seemed like no matter what day of the week or time of day, you would hit bumper-to-bumper traffic at that location. People heading to San Francisco would be in the San Jose or Hayward lanes, and cars going to Hayward would be in the San Francisco lane. This caused many last-minute lane changes, resulting in massive traffic jams.

Shakey was in no hurry. After being incarcerated for a year, time was now his friend. He didn't care how long it took to get "home." A free man never does, although he was amused by Nadine's impatience.

"You getting out or should I bring you a pillow and blanket?" Nadine smiled as she placed a hand on her hip.

"What, baby?" Shakey snapped out of his dream.

"Let's go in the house, love."

Shakey got out of the car and followed Nadine into her pad, greedily watching her ass wiggle from side to side with every step. Once they entered he noticed that everything looked as it had before. There were mirrored coffee and end tables, black with gold trim base, and a brown rent-to-own entertainment center holding a nineteen-inch color television along with VCR, turntable, dual cassette deck, and radio. Pictures of her family sat on top of that, plus assorted candles placed tastefully throughout the apartment. The sofa and love seat were brown leather, and on the wall above was a three-picture display of Martin, Malcolm, and Nelson.

On the opposite side of the room sat a brown baby grand piano decorated with multi-colored roses and family photos. Above was one of those old framed pictures of a white Jesus surrounded by scriptures. Black horizontal Venetian blinds and floor-to-ceiling gold-painted lamps completed her living room decor. Shakey went to sit on the sofa when Nadine slid into his arms and gave him a passionate kiss. His manhood began stiffening as her tongue swirled around inside his mouth.

Dropping to her knees, she jerked down his sweatpants and underwear with one pull and assaulted his meat. He stood, still lightly holding her head as it bobbed up and down, gobbling his pole like a lollipop. Gently nudging him back onto the couch, she worked him over for the next five minutes. By the time Nadine was done, Shakey was more than ready.

Heading for the bedroom, he disrobed as he walked. Nadine pulled her knit dress over her head, then slipped out of her pumps and panties as she followed him. Her mouth salivated as she admired his muscular build. By the time they reached the bedroom, Nadine was already hugging his back and lavishing kisses all over it.

Shakey turned around, bear-hugged Nadine, and kissed her with urgency. His manhood pressed on her belly, which caused her to begin a very sensuous grind. He matched her gyrations in intensity while gently laying her down on the bed. She lifted her legs up in the air and spread them as wide as she could. Shakey began gliding his meat up and down her slit, causing Nadine to soak his underside with juice.

Softly nibbling on her breasts, he penetrated, pushing his bone all the way in. She bit her bottom lip as he slammed in and out with the pent-up fury that incarceration will build up in a man. Nadine was in ecstasy. Shakey was the only man she'd ever known who could really ring her bell. He continued to plow deep inside her love canal and all she could do was accept it. The more he banged, the lower her legs dropped.

One thing about the Jones boys was they all carried big dicks, and Shakey was an expert cocksman. Changing his rhythm to a slow, sensuous stroke, he drove Nadine wild. Every muscle in her body was in use, and she felt sensations from her head down to her toes. What began as soft moans escaping her lips turned into cries of pleasure.

Once she started screaming, he shot off a hot, powerful blast of cream.

Holding each other like their lives depended on it, they lay entwined, falling into a peaceful sleep. After a few hours, Shakey woke up and went to take a shower. Nadine rolled over and gazed lovingly at "her man" then went to the closet. Shakey finished his bath and headed for the living room to put on his sweatsuit. Stopping in his tracks, he grinned from ear to ear while looking from Nadine to the living room and back again.

"Baby, what's this?" he asked.

"It's all for you, honey. My man has to look good."

Nadine had that schoolgirl look again as she beamed with pride. On the sofa, love seat, and across the dining room chairs lay an entire wardrobe for Shakey. She had bought him two Armani suits with matching Stacy Adams, underwear, socks, three nylon sweatsuits, matching tennis shoes, three pair of slacks, rayon shirts, cologne, hair dressing, lotion, two golf caps, and a godfather brim.

"You didn't have to do this," he said, knowing he would not let her take any of it back.

"Yes I did, baby—my man gone be looking good!!"

"Damn, this stuff must have set you back a pretty penny."

"Well, yes and no. You see, I like to call it an investment that will pay dividends. Plus, I can't be havin my man walking around in a too-small sweatsuit." They both laughed.

"I know that's right," he stated. "Come here."

Shakey embraced her and lavished kisses all over her face. Nadine felt on top of the world. At that moment she would do anything to please "her man."

"OK, what should I wear?" he asked while trying on his brim.

"I think a sweatsuit would look nice today."

"Good choice, baby. I'll wear the blue one. But first, I have something I need to do."

"What's that?" she asked.

Laying her down on the carpet, he mounted her. He was harder than a fifty-dollar jawbreaker and Nadine felt all his power. Lifting her legs high up in the air then forcing them down to her earlobes, he rammed his meat into her as hard as he could. Nadine's eyes rolled back into her head and she repeatedly called out his name. He was stretching her vagina to its limit and she was loving every minute of it.

Not having had sex for a year while "saving" herself for him, Nadine now felt like it was all worth it. He rode her the way a jockey rides a horse. Bouncing in and out, side to side, swirling around in circular motions, going slow, then fast, gentle, then furious, he spent every ounce of energy he had "springing her." When he finally came, she was "sprung."

"You want something to drink?" she asked in a husky voice.

"Yeah, what you got?"

"Water, orange juice, beer, and brandy," she responded.

"I'll take OJ."

"OK, let me get it for you."

Watching Nadine walk to the kitchen, Shakey smiled to himself. She was walking funny, almost sideways. He knew he'd hit that quat proper. He felt like a king. Before he was through with her, she would worship the ground he walked on, or so he thought. Taking the glass of juice from her, he gulped it down then headed back to the shower.

Shakey bathed then put on the aqua-blue sweatsuit Nadine laid out for him. After getting dressed and slapping on too much cologne, he spoke: "Let me use your ride. I need to make a couple of runs."

"OK, baby, the keys are on the coffee table."

"I'll be back as soon as I can but it might be a while."

"Where you got to go?"

"I gotta go to DMV and renew my license, the parole office, the police station, and visit a couple of homeboys."

"You want me to go with you?" she asked eagerly.

"Naw, you stay here and keep that pussy hot for me."

Kissing her on the lips, Shakey headed out the door while Nadine blushed from his last statement. When he returned she would be waiting for him to ring her bell some more. Putting Tony Toni Tone's "Thinking of You" into her sound system, Nadine began hanging up all the clothes she'd purchased for "her man."

Shakey backed out the driveway then headed down 73rd Avenue towards the Department of Motor Vehicles. Rolling past Eastmont Mall, he felt relieved to be free. He had so many things to do that he knew everything would not be accomplished in one day. At East 14th Street, 73rd turned into Hegenberger Road, which meant that the flow of traffic increased from thirty to forty-five miles an hour.

Hegenberger Road was a straight shot to the Oaktown Airport. The stretch from East 14th to the Coliseum consisted of four lanes in each direction with chain-link fences separating residents' backyards from the nonstop flow of traffic.

Shakey was amazed at all the changes that had occurred in one year. Where once there was nothing but the Coliseum, now the area was full of activity. Stores and restaurants saturated the landscape. On the right sat a huge Home Base Hardware store, Quality Tune-up, Denny's, and Sam's Hof-Brau. Across the street was a mini shopping center with Pak-n-Save, Taco Bell, and McDonald's.

Hooking a left at the corner, he drove past Arco, Shell, Jack in the Box, Holiday Inn, and Motel 6. Easing into the DMV's parking lot, he drove around scanning for an empty space. The lot was full as usual, but after his second go-round, he found a spot near the back of the lot.

The Department of Motor Vehicles, or DMV for short, was always crowded. Today would be no different. Once you entered, a long line greeted you at the front door leading up to the information/assistance desk. People sat on benches in front of the restrooms and next to the pay phones. The corner area was filled with test-takers hoping to renew or get that first driver's license. Long lines were formed at every window, with security guards watching all activity and California Highway Patrol officers coming in to take breaks, check license plates in the lot, or relieve themselves in the restroom.

"Next," the woman stated boldly.

"Yes, I'm here to renew my license," Shakey said.

"Do you have an appointment, sir?"

"No, I don't."

"Then you'll have to go to window B."

Shakey headed for the line at window B cursing to himself because he had just wasted twenty minutes waiting to be told something so simple. The line at window B would be longer, he knew, due to the fact that most people were required to explain why the hold or refusal for a license should be lifted. You also had one Latino trying to get eight California IDs for immigrants from Mexico who spoke little or no English.

Finally it was Shakey's turn. "Next in line, please."

"I'm here to renew."

"Do you have your license?" she asked.

"Yes, I do." Shakey handed it over.

After typing in information on the computer, the woman handed him back his expired license then told him, "Twelve dollars."

Shakey paid the fee, then the lady spoke again: "Fill out this form and go to window one."

The form she gave him was a change of address. He went to the next line. While waiting he noticed a strong aroma of funk coming from the man in front of him. The dude was dressed in a grease-stained blue mechanic's uniform with oily work boots. He wore a filthy beanie cap and had dirty fingernails. He turned around to Shakey and spoke.

"Man, these lines be too long."

"Oh yeah," Shakey responded.

"Shit yeah. I should'a mailed in my papers but I lagged on the shit. Now I'm stuck in this goddamn place when I could be out making money."

Shakey noticed that the man had several teeth missing,

and the ones he did have were yellow-brown. This resulted in a horrible odor emanating from his mouth. His nametag displayed the initials "DJ," and the longer they waited, the more strongly his scent permeated the air.

"You a mechanic, huh?" Shakey's tone was more a statement than a question.

"The best, bro—DJ Williams."

"Shakey." They gave each other a balled-up fist-over-fist greeting.

"How long you been fixing cars, DJ?"

"Man, I been working on cars all my life. Hell, I'll fix anythang."

"Oh yeah?"

"Shidd, they ain't built a car ol Dee cain't fix, shidd." DJ puffed out his chest.

"So you know about those computerized cars, huh?"

"Them new cars ain't shit. One thang go wrong and the whole car stops working. Only fools buy that shit! One, they made out of fiberglass, so if you in a wreck, you can kiss Christmas goodbye. Two, them little fools goin to school to learn about that shit cain't drop an engine the way I can. And three. . . . "

Before DJ could make his point, he was next up in line. Strolling up to window number four he passed Shakey his business card and told him, "If you ever need work done, bro, call me."

Shakey went to window number one while putting DJ's card in his pocket. The lady there was plump and pleasant. Around forty, she was dressed in blue jeans and a white blouse with flower designs. Glancing at her watch, she let out a sigh of relief because it was almost lunch-time.

"How may I help you, sir?"

"I'd like to renew my license," Shakey said while hand-ing her his license and change of address paper.

"Since you haven't had any violations, you don't have to take the written exam. However, if I could get you to step over to the chart, we can test your vision."

Shakey walked over to the line and covered each eye as she asked him to read off the letters. Although he was fudging and not fully covering one eye, the lady did not seem to care. Her mind was all set for lunch.

After passing the eye exam with flying colors, Shakey went to take his photo. The DMV employee peeled off a brown card then stamped it. Handing it to him she said, "Put this on the back of your license after you fill out the information on it. Your new license will be arriving in the mail within two to six weeks. Thank you, sir, and you have a nice day."

Shakey walked away grinning from ear to ear. Seeing DJ in the corner looking frustrated with his written exam, Shakey waved, displaying all thirty-two. DJ gave a half-hearted nod of the head then resumed the business at hand.

Getting in the Camaro, Shakey hit the down button on both windows. Putting a Digital Underground tape in the system, he cruised off bobbing his head to the "Humpty Dance" beat. Hooking a left on Hegenberger, he crossed over the freeway ramp then turned right on Edgewater Drive, a one-mile strip located in the industrial part of

town. The city's public works corps yard, an auto ware-
house, dental office, banks, service stations, various restaurants, and other small businesses littered the area.

Shakey drove past the Century movie complex and
eased into a parking lot. Taking off his sweat jacket, he
strutted into Alameda County's parole office. The receptionist, a young Latina, was putting a file in the cabinet
with her back turned. Glancing at Shakey, she spoke:
"Have a seat—I'll be with you in a minute."

Shakey did as instructed but his steely gaze remained
zoomed in on the female. She wore a red dress that hugged
her awesome frame, and thick black hair cascaded down
her back. Blue pumps along with dark lipstick and hairy
bare legs aroused Shakey instantly. His manhood filled
with blood as he squirmed in his seat.

"How may I help you?"

"Can I tell the truth?" he flirted.

"Let me put it another way—who would you like to
see?"

"I'm looking at her."

"OK, now that you saw, what do you really want?"

"Can I tell the truth?"

"No, tell a lie," she laughed.

Shakey sighed, and as he rolled his eyes, she shot a
glance at his crotch then looked away embarrassed. Her
riveting black eyes bore into his as she picked at her nose,
hoping he would notice her wedding band.

"Oh, I see, you married, huh?"

"Happily."

"Well, cain't blame a brother for trying."

"Thank you, now let's start over." She was relieved.

"My name is Calvin Jones and I'm here to see Mr. Johnson."

"Do you have an appointment?"

"No, I was just released this morning."

"I'm sorry, but Mr. Johnson is out for the rest of the day. Let me schedule you."

Flipping the pages of her reservation book, she said, "I have an opening for next Tuesday at two P.M."

"That's cool."

"OK, Mr. Jones, we'll see you then."

"You sho will." He flashed a smile.

"Bye, Mr. Jones." She was smiling too.

Shakey strutted out the door boldly, pausing as it closed and turning around. The receptionist jerked her head down and began shuffling papers. Laughing, he spoke to himself: *"Yeah, she's curious. Shakey boy, you still got it."*

Shakey was like most other men, thinking a woman liked him when she didn't. He wasn't aware of the fact that sexual harassment charges lurked in the workplace like flies on shit. He got in Nadine's car full of himself and headed for 880.

The Nimitz Freeway, a.k.a. 880, was its usual congested self, with big rigs dominating. By the time he realized that traffic was approaching a virtual standstill, it was too late—he was part of the mess. Remaining in the right lane, he exited at Sixty-Sixth; from there he would take the streets.

Deciding to take East 14th, he hooked a left at Havenscourt Junior High and rolled. Block after block he saw that things here hadn't changed much. East 14th was still run-down until you approached High Street. There, Mexican-owned businesses were booming all the way to Twenty-Third Avenue.

As he drove he noticed that each street sign displayed not only the crossing avenue name along with East 14th, but above that sign sat another that read "INTERNA-TIONAL Boulevard."

Wondering why East 14th had signs above it saying INTERNATIONAL, he realized that the area from 14th to 1st (Lake Merritt) was on hits with Chinese business.

"Where in the hell are the black businesses?" he growled to himself.

Taking 12th Street to Clay, he hooked a left down to Seventh, made another left, then parked. Getting out, he walked into the police department.

OPD headquarters, as usual, bustled with activity. The place swarmed with cops, attorneys, prisoners, citizens, and the homeless. Shakey got in line at the front desk and waited his turn. There were two black officers answering any and all questions. Easing up to the counter, he said, "Yeah, I'm here to register."

"Take the elevator to the third floor, room 313," responded the muscular officer.

"Thanks."

Shakey rode up to the third floor and entered room 313. Relieved to see the place deserted, he went to the counter. The lady at the desk saw him come in, so she got out of her seat and asked him while he was still walking to the window, "May I help you, sir?"

"Yes, I'm here to register," he said while pulling out his papers.

"Do you have an appointment?"

"Nobody told me I needed one."

"Well, we no longer take walk-ins, but I can schedule you."

"OK, that'll work."

"Let me get my book."

She went to get her appointment calendar while Shakey took in the sight. The lady was both pleasant and phine, dressed in hip-hugging black jeans with a black turtleneck sweater displaying OPD IDENTIFICATION UNIT on the collar. He was drooling at the mouth.

While she scanned her book for an open date, Shakey noticed that the office was full of phine women all dressed in jeans. He was unaware of the fact that it was dress-down Friday. Actually, he didn't care because he was getting an eyeful.

"Damn, they got some phine-ass women in here," he thought to himself.

"OK, sir, I can schedule you for next Tuesday at eight-thirty."

"Good, that means I get to see you again."

"You need to quit it," she laughed.

"I'm serious, what's yo name?"

"OK, next Tuesday at eight-thirty." She ignored his play.

Folding up his papers while feeling stupid, Shakey headed out the door. Before he could leave the office, one of the ladies came from the back and said, "Earlene, you have a call on line two."

Shakey turned around grinning at her while repeatedly whispering "Earlene" and nodding his head. Earlene saw him and without cracking a smile said, "Goodbye, Mr. Jones."

"Bye, EARLENE." He laughed out loud.

Entering the hallway, he spotted a sister glancing at her watch. She appeared pressed for time. She wore a matching purple two-piece skirt set with legs that were sculpted. Her hair streamed down her back to just below the shoulders, and she was very pretty. But those legs would stop traffic and cause accidents on the rainiest of days.

"How ya doin?" Shakey asked.

"Hello," she responded.

"Do you know how phine you are?"

She ignored him.

"Damn, baby, I dream about women like you. My name is Shakey, what's yours?"

She ignored him.

"Oh, you stuck-up, huh?"

Just as her lips were forming to tell him off, a fly brother strolled out the restroom. He was decked out in a black tailor-made Italian suit with shoes shining so bright you could see your reflection. Walking up to Shakey's object of desire, he stated, "I'm sorry, but I had to finish my paperwork. Hope we're not late."

"I hope so too," she smiled.

Shakey rode the elevator with them, disappearing towards the back. Seeing OPD badges on them both, he thought to himself, *"Damn, phine-ass broad a goddamn cop. That fool is too. Dey do look good together, though."*

The couple hurriedly exited the station while Shakey lagged behind purposely. If he couldn't have her, he was damn sure gonna get his money's worth looking. She was all that, then some.

Feeling hungry, he put coins in the parking meter then walked two blocks to Nation's to grab a bite to eat. Ordering a cheeseburger, fries, and large Coke, he ate in silence while watching all the beautiful women come and go.

Leaving his mess on the table, he went back to the car and drove to the west side. He thought about calling Nadine, then thought the better of it. He would not be reporting his whereabouts to any woman. Pulling up in front of Chestnut Court, he got out.

Chestnut Court, situated on the west side, was a government housing project that resembled a fortress. The only good thing people said about this complex that spanned six city blocks was that it had an excellent city-run childcare center. While peaceful in the day, Chestnut Court was a war zone at night. Teenagers dominated, selling drugs, harassing tenants, fighting, loitering, and having a good time.

Shakey remembered the three-story-high court as being painted beige; now it was lavender with purple trim. There was only one drive-in entrance, but you could walk in from anywhere. Jogging up the stairs, he went to a third-floor unit and rang the bell.

Yolanda heard the bell ring, then got up from the kitchen table while telling her friend Sheila, "Hold on girl, let me get the doe."

"It's alright, take your time!" Shakey blurted through the screen.

"Now, there's only one man I know who can talk shit like that to me and get away with it. And he's locked up," she said.

"Well, as you know, they cain't keep a playa down fa long." He was grinning.

"Shakey? Damn, you out?"

"Hell yeah, I'm out. Now let me in foe dey lock my ass up again!"

Yolanda opened the door and bear-hugged Shakey. They embraced as if they were long-lost relatives reunited.

"Girl, you still look good, even after all those kids," he stated.

"Yeah, and yo eyes still brown."

"My eyes still brown?" he asked.

"Yes, dear, full of shit!" she laughed.

"Well I see you ain't lost yo dream."

"And what dream would that be, dear?"

"Ta be a comedienne!" He grabbed his stomach and let out a hearty laugh.

"Aw fuck you, niggah! Slack, baby, come here for a minute!" she hollered out.

Slack lazily wandered out of the bedroom, then rubbed his eyes and took a second look. Breaking out in a hearty grin that only true friends know, he embraced Shakey.

Robert "Slack" Henderson was Shakey's lifelong right-hand man. Six foot even, cream-colored and skinny, Slack didn't strike fear with his size. What people feared was the fact Slack would kill you and get away with it. He was a professional hit man.

The police labeled him the Oaktown Devil because they knew he'd committed several homicides over the years but had never been charged with anything. He never left a usable clue, and he didn't have diarrhea of the mouth. He wouldn't even tell Yolanda the details of his crimes.

"Damn, boy, you must'a got out early!" Slack's teeth were on full display.

"Yeah, man—you know it." Shakey's smile was sincere.

"My boy Shake, back on the block! Come on, let's go in my room."

They headed back to Slack's bedroom while Yolanda whispered to her friend what a great dude Shakey was. Slack closed the door, then turned serious.

"Dude, you need a piece?" he asked.

"Naw gee, I'mo play it straight for a while, see what happens," Shakey responded.

"What about funds?"

"I'm on empty."

"Well, we gone hafta do somethin 'bout that."

"What I really want is to find that fool named Rainbow and peel his cap."

"Consider it done." Slack was serious.

"What you got good?" Shakey asked.

"Man, I got the bomb. That sticky shit."

"What you waitin for, fool, light that shit up!" They both laughed.

"Awight, let's party then."

They gave each other a solid brotherhood handshake, then returned to the living room with Shakey firing up a joint of weed.

"Sheila, this is Shakey, Slack's ace coon boon. Shakey,

meet my girl Sheila," Yolanda said with pride.

"Hello." Sheila rose as she spoke and extended her hand.

"Hey, how you doin" was all Shakey could come up with.

Sheila Duncan was tall and willowy. Standing six two, she looked Shakey directly in the eye. Her hair was pulled back into a bun so it was hard to tell how much she had, but Shakey didn't even notice. He was too busy sizing up her frame.

Her butterscotch complexion, small nose, full lips covered with red lipstick, and catlike eyes intrigued him. She wore a sky-blue summer dress with straps on the shoulders and a split on the side. Costume jewelry, fake fingernails, and blue open-toed shoes completed her get-up.

She was skinny like Olive Oyl but the girl had hips, a nice ass, and long legs that looked delicious. Shakey couldn't complain. She spoke again while still holding his hand.

"I'm doing fine, but I bet you being free makes you feel like you're doing better than me." Her voice was soft and sensuous.

"Maybe so, but if I had you, we'd both be in love." Everyone laughed.

"How long were you away?" Sheila continued.

"Too long, but if I'da known 'Lon had a friend like you, I would'a made the Man let me out a long time ago."

"Oh, really?" She was blushing now.

"If I'm lyin, I'm flyin. Tell me 'bout yo self."

"What would you like to know?"

"You got a man?"

"No, but I do have a friend."

"Aw shit, here we go with that 'I got a friend' shit."

"I'm just telling the truth," she smiled, displaying even teeth.

"How long you and this here friend been seeing each other?"

"I've known Marcus for about a year, and it's not what you think."

"Oh, you just met me and know what I think already?"

"No, but men always think a woman can't have a male friend without there being hanky panky!" She was direct.

"Girl, give me a hug."

He released her hand and she slid into his arms. Slack and Yolanda both watched with sheepish grins on their faces. After half a minute, Shakey released her and Sheila sat back down. Then he resumed his rap.

"Well, tell everybody you got a new friend now."

"OK," she whispered as she thought of how strong his body felt.

Shakey relit the burned-out joint, took a long drag, then passed it to Sheila.

"Man, how you gone be givin my shit to her?" Slack asked, looking dumbfounded.

"Niggah, if you passed my weed ta 'Lon I wouldn't say shit and you know it," Shakey grinned as he eyed Sheila.

"Damn, muafucka just gone gib mah shit ta somebody else. Shake, let's go to da sto—I need a drank after all this drama."

"I'll be right back, baby," Shakey told Sheila.

"OK." She felt important.

"Baby, yaw need anythang?" Slack asked Yolanda.

"No dear, we're fine," she returned.

"Yeah, yaw sho is," Shakey blurted out while zooming in on Sheila.

Sheila passed the weed to Yolanda and they both cracked up. Satisfied with his game, Shakey headed for the door, winking at Sheila on the way out. She blushed and waved. Heading down the stairwell, Shakey and Slack heard the women roaring with laughter.

"Slack, baby, that girl is mine."

"Oh, you know that, huh?"

"Hell yeah, man. Dude, you seen the way she was lookin at me?"

"Yeah, you got a point, Shake."

They got in Slack's bucket and sped off. The car was a beige '82 Corolla four-door. It had dents and looked ugly but ran like a champ.

"Awight, gimme da lowdown," Shakey said, still focused on the latest woman.

"Sheila's good people, dude—two kids, never had a man worf a damn, and low self-esteem."

"What about finances?"

"She gets Section 8, works, drives that red Hyundai over there, and dresses nice. Her height scares most of the riffraff away."

"Height don't mean shit to a niggah like me, shidd. Once I get through with her, she gonna thank she ten foot tall anyway," he bragged.

Slack pulled up in front of the store smiling at Shakey's braggadocio. They both got out and walked into the small, poorly stocked business. The liquor refrigerators were full and cigarettes were plentiful, but the shelves were nearly bare of other essentials.

Grabbing two fifths of Thunderbird, Slack set the bottles on the counter. While he fished for his money, two little nappy-headed boys came in the door selling candy for their basketball team. Shakey watched the scene with more than a passing interest.

"Mohammed, would you like to buy some candy so we can get our basketball uniforms?" the kid asked.

"No, why should I buy candy from jew when I sell candy?" Mohammed laughed.

"Aw, fuck dis towel-on-his-head-wearin punk, James, let's go," said the bigger kid.

"Jew get your ass outta my store!"

"See, that's why y'all have no respect from my people," Shakey said while staring the store owner down.

"My prend, what are jew talking about?"

"I ain't yo friend and what I'm talking about is you not buying candy from these dudes."

"I no need candy."

"Dat ain't the point. The point is black people spend money with you each and every day, yet you put nothing back into the black community. You overcharge for everything in dis hole-in-da-wall, den send for some moe of yo gaddamn people to come here on da boat!" Shakey was angry.

"Jew an jo prend, jew leeb," he said to Slack.

"Aw, fuck you, you goddamn Arab," said Shakey as he stormed out glaring at Mohammed. Reaching into his pocket, he then bought five bars of candy from the youngsters, gave each one two bars and ripped off the paper from the remaining candy bar. Taking a bite, he threw the rest of it on the ground right in front of the door.

Mohammed wanted to say something, but noticing Shakey's well-chiseled body along with his bluntness of action, he kept his mouth shut. The men got in the car and peeled rubber.

"Dude, you still a fool," Slack joked.

"I ain't did shit but assaulted his conscious level," Shakey smiled.

They rode three blocks laughing about Shakey's temper tantrum. He took Slack's good-natured ribbing in stride. Slack eased his bucket into the driveway of a house on Union Street and they both got out.

The house was right across the street from Poplar Recreation Center in an area of the city known as "Dogtown." Like many of the homes in this poverty-filled neighborhood, it was in desperate need of repair. Painted beige with an ugly brown trim, it was shabby. There was no porch—just three concrete steps that were cracked. There were no railings, either. The front door was rotted wood surrounding filthy window squares. The yard was mostly dirt with a few patches of grass. Motor oil stains, trash, and broken glass littered the lot.

They walked up the three-stepped porch and Slack rang the buzzer. After the second ring, a frail older woman peered through the curtains. Opening the door, she gave Slack a hug then spoke.

"Shakey, is dat you?" She squinted her eyes.

"Yes, it's me! How ya doin, Miss McKnight?" He hugged her.

"I'm alright, jus get kinda lonely sometimes wit Spodie bein dead an all."

"Yeah I know, it's been a bad year for us all," Shakey stated solemnly.

"Bad ain't da word. You know I seed dat boy Rainbow go in da garage, den da police ketch 'im red-handed aftah he done kilt mah boy. So ah looks into da car an he cain't eben look me back, den ah knowed he did it. Da nex day dey let his black ass go free cause dey don't care nuttin 'bout mah baby, so I say ta da big black officer dat dey knowed dey was wrong lettin dat fool go cause he kilt mah son, and dey say dey couldn't prove it. Den I say dey didn't wanna prove it. Den he try ta say James been dead long time foe dat niggah showed up, so ah say det dat shit ain't right cause he did it den came back ta finish da job. Ah say everybody knows dat mah boy kept money hid inside dose cars he be workin on, den dey try ta say"

"Mama McKnight, I came ta show Shakey the car he was gonna buy from Spodie," Slack interrupted her.

He'd heard the same story at least a hundred times and wasn't about to listen to it again. James "Spodie" Mc-Knight was Mattie McKnight's only child. He was found beaten to death and Rainbow standing over his body holding the baseball bat.

Because Rainbow had an airtight alibi and had in fact shown up at Spodie's garage long after the crime was committed by someone else, the police were forced to release him, which further damaged their credibility with

Dogtown residents. As far as the people were concerned, Rainbow was caught red-handed holding the murder weapon.

Slack and Shakey walked out of the house and went out back to the garage. Slack unlocked the door using the key that had been in his possession since Spodie's murder. Turning on the light, they entered the musty room temporarily holding their breath.

Car parts, motor oil, tires, and tools were scattered around carelessly. Old car seats lined the walls, and a mini refrigerator sat unplugged in the corner. A beat-up Caddy covered with dust occupied the center of the room.

The garage was ice-cold but neither man seemed to notice. Slack unlocked the padlocks under the front grill then got in the car and pulled the hood release knob. Shakey raised it up while his partner began unscrewing the wing-nut over the distributor cap.

Slack grabbed the air filter, turned it over, then lifted off the black rubber cover. The lining had been carved out and replaced by stacks of money and base rock. The bills were neatly wrapped in rubber bands, and the dope was packed in ziplock bags.

"Damn, man, how much is dat?" Shakey asked, looking on in amazement.

"You got fourteen G's plus seven in dope."

"Shidd, I'm da fuckin man, den."

"Yeah dude, you da man," Slack grinned.

"Slack, you awight. You could'a cheated me fa hella dis, but you didn't. See das what ahm talkin 'bout, shidd!" Shakey gave Slack a bear hug.

"Why would I cheat you, homes? You mah boy," Slack cheesed.

"Hell yeah, I'm yo muthafuckin boy, shidd! Now ah know ahmo get Sandra back, cause we bofe know she money-hungry!" They laughed.

"Dude, look," Shakey continued, "ahmo take half a dis and leave da rest."

Slack nodded in agreement as Shakey put half the money and dope in a paper bag. They returned the rest to its original hiding place, with Slack padlocking the hood. Turning off the lights, they closed the door and left. Slack walked up to Mama McKnight's door and told her that the car needed more work before it could be moved, so they would be back in a few days.

Shakey waved at her from the driveway then got in the car. Opening a bottle of T-bird and taking a swig, Slack backed out and sped off with the open container of alcohol in his lap. He always rode this way.

After easing into Slack's assigned spot at the "court," they got out. Shakey stuffed a wad of cash into his pocket then told Slack to tell Sheila he would call her. They gave each other a brotherhood hug, and Shakey drove off in Nadine's car. Sheila was disappointed to not see him in person, but she hoped Shakey would call soon.

6
SO IN LOVE

Cassandra walked down the long hallway of Simplicity Recording Studio noticing all the framed and autographed photos of the many artists who had recorded there. Rappers dominated, most of whom were unfamiliar to her. She liked jazz music and so did her man, for that matter.

How he could be a rapper was a marvel to her, when he hated the false braggadocio, the put-down of women, and profanity-laced lyrics that most of the rap artists produced. Since he always refused to bust a rhyme in public, she had no idea what to expect today. His excuse was that he wanted to "surprise" her.

She was dressed in loose-fitting blue jeans, white and blue striped oversized sweater, white lowtop jogging sneakers, and a powder-blue golf cap. Her extension braids covered both sides of her face, along with dark-colored lipstick accenting her midnight-black complexion.

No one noticed as she quietly entered the room because everyone's eyes were riveted on the recording booth. The room was larger than you would imagine from the outside. Three beat-up brown leather sofas were situated along different walls. All were occupied by happy faces—some she knew, others she didn't. An ice cooler sat off to the side filled with beer and bottled water. A worn-out table was laden with fruit and hors d'oeuvre trays covered with everything from finger sandwiches to cheeses, sliced pastrami, turkey, ham, dry salami, roast beef, crackers, peppers, watermelon, kiwi, oranges, cherry tomatoes, grapes, and olives.

The beat was thumping and the rapper was deep into his cut. As it vamped out, Cassandra's head was rocking right along with everyone else's, and she had to admit that her man sounded wonderful. His rhymes were educational and full of wisdom. Cassandra was beyond impressed; she was ecstatic.

Rainbow exited the booth and flicked off the "recording" light switch. Waving at his honey, he headed for the engineers who were manning the master control board. They were two young fly-looking brothers who appeared to know exactly what they were doing.

"How'd it sound, Vern?" Rainbow asked the younger of the two.

"It was fly, 'Bo, but."

"But what, Vern? I knew I should have asked JP!" They all laughed.

"You asked for a hit, dude. A hit I can't help you with

when we have if, ands, or buts. Now one more voiceover should do the trick."

Vern left no doubt that they would record some more. He was always matter-of-fact with his convictions. Decked out in beige Stacy Adams boots with matching socks, slacks, and rayon shirt, he was definitely fly. Gold rings, ropes, bracelets, and a fine quartz timepiece on his wrist accented his attire. Vern stood five eleven, one-sixty, but appeared to be much thinner. His complexion was as bright as a dull light bulb, in stark contrast to his jet-black hair.

Johnny P, on the other hand, was blue-black—so dark that his face always appeared shiny like a pair of slacks worn day after day. Six foot one and weighing two-ten, JP was powerfully built. He was dressed in a royal blue V-neck sweater with matching slacks, no socks, and blue shoes.

A thick rope hung from his neck with a medallion displaying "JP." He wore a California Curl hairdo with so much spray that it dripped constantly, staining any and everything. JP was Rainbow's dj, and his skills were unmatched. The boy was as good as it gets. Scratching, dubbing, sampling, it didn't matter—if JP couldn't do, it couldn't be done. Blue-black was the best in the west.

Rainbow didn't seem to mind the extra work at all. He was like a kid in a candy store. Five foot eleven inches tall with broad shoulders and a solid build, he was handsome. Decked out in a black Nike sweatsuit, no shirt, Kangol safari hat, and black Air Jordans, he looked the part of a rapper personality. He wore huge rings on his fingers, along with a phat gold rope around his neck.

Grabbing a bottle of water out of the cooler, he asked Vern, "So what you want me ta do, gee?"

"'Bo, we need to start at the part about Abraham Lincoln and go until the KKK."

"Alright, dude, just give me about five minutes with my people."

"Yeah, man." Vern was preoccupied with the mixing board.

Rainbow headed for the crowd of smiling faces, happily accepting all the pats on the back and declarations of a hit song in the making. After a couple of minutes, he made his way to his honey.

"Hey, baby, what do you think?" he said while kissing her.

"Baby, I didn't know you could rap like that!" She was impressed.

"Well, there's a lot of things about me you'll find out in due time, girl."

"Is that so?"

"Yeah, baby, it's so, but anyway, I have to do a voiceover and hang around while Vern and JP master the track."

"How long will that take?"

"I don't know, probably about three hours. Look, you can go home and I'll be there when we're done."

"OK. Did you want me to pack your bags too?" she asked.

"Pack my bags?" He was lost.

"Honey . . . you remember when I told you about the overnighter party bus to Reno?"

"Yeah, I remember now. Damn, what time you say that

bus is leaving?" he asked, stroking his chin.

"It's leaving at seven, babes."

"Alright, that gives me at least a few hours' sleep. OK, baby, let me move this program along."

Rainbow gave Cassandra a quick peck on the lips and in the next instant was conversing with Vern and JP. She eased out the door while he entered the booth.

Cassandra had been Rainbow's woman for three months now. While driving home she thought about the things she loved about him. He was a good provider, generous to a fault, and loved her. Although they'd only known each other briefly, she felt comfortable leaving her apartment to move in with him.

Pulling up in the driveway of her new home, she pushed the remote and the garage door opened. She exited through the side door and "Iceberg" bum-rushed her.

"Woof, woof!" His tail was wagging.

"Hey 'Berg, how ya doin, baby?" she cooed, rubbing his neck.

"Woof."

Iceberg was Rainbow's purebred German shepherd whom he named after the player "Iceberg Slim." He was jet-black on top with gold legs and underside. He also had a few splotches of gold around the eyes and ears.

"Come on, 'Berg, let me give you some water."

Iceberg followed Cassandra to the water dish with his tail wagging and tongue dripping saliva. She turned on the hose and filled his bowl while he lapped greedily. Upon finishing, she went into the house.

Cassandra had just recently agreed to move in with her

man, which meant giving up her own place. It was only a matter of time before they got married anyway. She loved her new home and her new man.

The home was a single-level two-bedroom with potential. Painted money-green with white trim, it had space for room additions or building upwards. The yard was nicely manicured, and like most homes on the block, neat in appearance.

Located on the east side, Agua Vista was a two-block row of homes where the homeowners cared. They held block parties and neighborhood watch meetings, posted reward signs for lost or stolen dogs, and everyone who lived on the block knew everyone else. That in itself was a soap opera.

Cassandra had big plans for her new place. She thought the house would look better in a color scheme of sky blue with white trim. A six-foot chain-link fence wouldn't be a bad idea, either. She had already persuaded Rainbow to repave the driveway, along with installing an electric garage door.

Entering the bedroom, she tossed two suitcases on the bed and began riffling through closets and drawers. One hour later, their luggage was packed and the room was clean. She took a shower and went to bed, setting the alarm clock for five-thirty.

Rainbow walked in at six, inhaling fumes from the bacon Cassandra was frying. Realizing that he wouldn't get any sleep, he took a shower then dressed. They sat at the table and held hands while Cassandra blessed the food. Once they were done, Cassandra locked the doors while

Rainbow hoisted the suitcases into the trunk of the car. "Bertha" was a green Honda Accord with all the trimmings. They drove a short distance to meet the Reno bus at Eastmont Mall and pulled into a parking stall. The mall wouldn't open until nine, so the parking lot was deserted. They got out and Cassandra headed towards the bus driver, while Rainbow followed with their stuff.

After Cassandra motioned to him to confirm that the bus was theirs, he placed their cases into one of the luggage compartments on the side. Rainbow had never been on a party bus to Reno, so he had no idea what to expect.

They walked past the crowd milling in front of the door and stepped up into the coach. It was a forty-seven-passenger, plush from top to bottom. Cassandra handed over the tickets to a lady on the top step and waved greetings to all the smiling faces she knew on board.

Rainbow followed her on and was surprised at what he saw. On the front passenger seat sat a large ice cooler filled with several types of beer, soda, and bottled water, along with ice. Next to that, a small box sat displaying brandy, gin, vodka, and cognac. Stuffed in between the box and the cooler were straws, napkins, and cups. On the opposite seat, directly behind the driver, were four extra-large aluminum pans covered with foil. Pens, pads, styrofoam trays, cassettes, and videotapes littered the remaining space.

Taking an aisle seat next to Cassandra in the middle of the bus, Rainbow looked up and noticed miniature televisions situated on the ceiling playing a music video. Glancing around, he noticed that many of the people were drinking already, at seven in the morning.

The bus eased off while everyone was handed a styro-foam tray. Next, the trip sponsors lined themselves up assembly-style and began passing the large pans down the aisle while people fixed their plates.

One tray was filled to the brim with fried chicken drummettes. The next had rows of dry salami, roast beef, pressed ham, and turkey piled in mounds. There were also rows of American and Swiss cheese, along with snack crackers. The third pan was the veggie tray, consisting of tomato slices, Greek peppers, olives, green onions, and celery. The final tray had watermelon squares, orange and kiwi slices, grapes, strawberries, and cherries.

Rainbow found this to be impressive. However, since he'd just eaten his BLT sandwich, he wasn't really hungry. He got a few pieces of chicken along with some deli meat and olives, then closed his tray and placed it in the compartment above his head.

"So babes, what do you think?" Cassandra asked.

"It's cool—they got a nice hookup."

"Let me introduce you to my folks." Looking around, Cassandra continued, "Rainbow, this is Lorraine and next to her, that's Ramona. Over there are Greg and Mary, and right in front of them are Howard and Jeanette. Everybody, this is the love of my life, Reggie, but we call him Rainbow."

"Rainbow?" Lorraine piped up. "How did you get a name like that?"

"Well, it's my rap tag. Hopefully, one day it will be a household name."

"Oh, I see. So you're the reason we don't see Sandy anymore?"

"You could say that."

"OH KAY!" Lorraine gave Ramona five.

Rainbow leaned back in his seat and started watching the music videos. Out of the corner of his eye, he noticed Lorraine stealing glances. She was in the aisle seat directly across from him.

Lorraine Tucker was thick, loud, and a troublemaker. Rainbow knew the type, so he knew she was bad news. He assumed that she wanted to see if he would play in order to slander Cassandra's name at work. Wearing a very short green skirt with matching halter top, she displayed her frame like a model on the runway. Every chance she got, she was getting up to go to the restroom, to the front of the bus, or just to pull her skirt down. The girl was phine, knew it, but wanted Rainbow to notice. He played sleep.

The tour director, Lucille, got on the microphone announcing the "time game." This required you to bet a dollar to guess what time the bus pulled up at the first casino. You could make more than one guess if you wanted, but each choice costed a buck.

"Baby, give me five dollars," Cassandra said.

"Five for what?" Rainbow groggily inquired.

"For the time game, Rainbow!" Cassandra said incredulously.

"Here." He handed it over.

Rainbow gave her the money then shut his eyes once again. He attempted to get some sleep but every few minutes, Cassandra would wake him wanting money for the bingo game, raffle tickets, and bus driver donation. It was more like each hour, but Rainbow was so exhausted from the overnight recording session that he regretted ever agreeing to come on the trip.

The bus pulled up in front of the Virginian Casino in downtown Reno. There a representative got on and gave each passenger a ten-dollar redemption coupon and drink ticket, along with other discounts. The passengers disembarked and the bus rolled off.

"Hey, I didn't get the luggage," Rainbow stated.

"Baby . . . stop making a spectacle of yourself!" she whined.

"Doing what?"

"Look honey, the bus comes back in three hours, then we get the rooms."

"Oh." He scratched his head.

"Now let's go cash these."

She stormed into the casino with her man following closely behind. Riding the escalator up to the second floor, they got in line and redeemed their coupons. Cassandra got ten bo-dollars while Rainbow got a ten-dollar bill. He walked with her to the gaming area and pulled up a stool next to the dollar slot machine she chose.

She dropped three coins into the machine, which was the maximum, and lost. Two more pulls had her reaching for her purse. She called over a change maker and gave the lady a hundred-dollar bill for five twenty-dollar rolls of coins. Rainbow watched in amazement as she lost that hundred, then two more. They still had two hours to go before the bus took them to their room, and she was broke already.

"Let's go get something to eat," he suggested.

"Damn, baby, you see how close I was! That shit was seven-seven-cherry—damn!" She was focused on the machine.

"Alright, let's go eat." He pulled her up from the stool and took her to the snack bar.

"Two chili cheese dogs and two colas," he ordered as he handed over the ducats.

The cook handed Rainbow and Cassandra the chili cheese plates along with the drinks. Rainbow headed straight for the condiment section and added onions, jalapeno peppers, and tomatoes. She followed him to a table and picked at her food while he ate like a man starving.

"Baby, you ain't eatin?" he asked.

"I really don't have an appetite."

"This shit on hits, gurll!"

Rainbow devoured all of his meal then ate Cassandra's too. The hot dogs were smothered with chili beans with cheese generously sprinkled on top. Everybody knows that in Reno, the food is practically given away, so all the servings are on hits.

Since they still had an hour before the bus returned to take them to their room, Rainbow told Cassandra, "Let's go next door to Cal Neva."

"For what?" She had a nastiness in her voice that he didn't like.

"So I can bet on some college and pro football games. I play parley, baby."

"Par who?" She was curious.

"Parley."

"What is that?"

"That's where I make my money. What I do is bet the odds."

They rode the escalators up to the third floor of the Cal Neva Casino, where Rainbow walked to the counter and grabbed a handful of parley sheets. Next he began explaining the game to his woman.

"As you can see, they have listed every game, college and pro. Each team has a number, along with a number for the over/under."

"Each team has a number?" She was lost.

"Yes, baby. Take, for example, the Raiders against Dallas. The Cowboys are seven-and-a-half-point favorites so that means if you pick them, they have to win by eight points in order for you to collect."

"What if they don't do that?"

"If they win by seven points or less, then the winning team is the Raiders as far as betting is concerned."

"So let me see if I got this straight, Rainbow. I think Dallas is going to win the game, but if they only win by three points, then I lose my money even though they won the game?"

"Exactly," Rainbow answered.

"That's stupid!" she retorted.

"No, it is not—those are the rules. Anyway, number 79 is for Dallas, 80 for the Raiders, the point spread is there right next to their names. Now you darken in your selection at the bottom just like you would a lottery game.

The over/under numbers for each game are listed right below."

"Wait a minute—over/under, what's that?" she asked, irritated.

"You see, number 81 says over forty-one and a half, 82 says under forty-one and a half."

"Yes, I see that," she interrupted.

"Alright baby, say the score is something like 21 to 18."

"For who?" she butted in again.

"It doesn't matter who, 21 plus 18 equals 39, and since that's under forty-one and a half, the people who choose 'under' win that bet."

"So how much do you win?"

"It all depends on how many selections you make," he said while flipping over the card. "See baby, if you bet three picks and all three picks win, that pays you six dollars for every dollar you bet, six-to-one odds. Four picks is eleven to one, twenty-six for five, all the way up to twenty-five thousand to one for fifteen right picks."

"You have to get all fifteen right though, huh?" She spoke in a negative tone. "I think this is a bigger risk than the slots—at least you can win *sometimes*. With this game, you may not win a bet. Baby, I gotta go to the restroom."

She bounced while Rainbow marked his cards. He bet a hundred dollars on Green Bay, Dallas, and Buffalo. He also bet a fifty-spot on UCLA, Washington, and Florida State. Upon receiving his free drink coupons, Rainbow picked out a space at the bar counter, since all the tables were taken.

Before he sat down he realized that he had to urinate. Wandering around, he peeped out the restrooms. Right before he got there, he glanced left down the escalator and saw Cassandra at an ATM machine. Standing off to the side he viewed as she withdrew what appeared to be a fat stack of twenties.

Rainbow entered the restroom and relieved himself of his bodily fluids, then washed his hands and walked back out, returning to his spot. The sports and race book area is where the big spenders resided. You could bet on all the big-time fights, the major sports, hockey, golf, tennis, and horse racing from around the world. Side-by-side television monitors completely surrounded the room showing college football games, hockey, boxing, and horse racing from around the country. Every now and then the majority of players would scream out, usually when a game neared its conclusion and everything was academic. The roar usually came after a game-winning or -losing score, fumble, or interception.

Sitting down to watch college ball, Rainbow thought about his woman. She played lottery daily, bingo nightly, and went on someone's Reno bus monthly. The few times she'd won, she would lose it all over the span of a few days, often asking for what she'd given him back. Now he knew why her cash flow was always short: she was hooked on gambling.

Rainbow walked back over to the betting window and handed the teller another card. He selected Miami, Florida, Oklahoma, Nebraska, and UCLA. Betting twenty dollars, he received his ticket along with two free drink coupons and returned to his seat. This five-team wager would return him five hundred dollars, and since all his choices were college heavyweights, he felt like his chances were good. Pre-season college ball was overloaded with mismatches where the dominant teams were often favored by forty points or more. There was no doubt who would win, only by how much. The scores were always astronomical, with numbers like 70 to 3.

Cassandra returned with the look of a loser.

"Damn, I'm glad it's almost time for the bus to come—I'm ready ta go," she said.

"How'd you do?" he asked.

"I did alright."

"How much you ahead?"

"They got about two hundred of my money, but I'll win it back tonight." she lied. "How you doin?"

"I won't know until the games are over, but my early game picks are all kickin ass," he bragged.

"Good for you, baby. Let's go catch the bus to the rooms." She wasn't excited.

They went outside to the parked bus, which was fifty percent occupied. The losing faces on the bus depressed Rainbow. He wondered how they could get broke in three hours knowing they would be here until tomorrow. The winning players were the last to board, getting on holding cups full of money or liquor, or eating while bragging about what they did.

Lorraine and Ramona entered and strutted to their seats holding large cups filled with bo-dollars.

"Girl, what you do?" Lorraine asked Cassandra.

"Oh, we didn't do no serious gambling yet," she lied.

"Gurll, me and Mona popped dat ass!"

"Yaw did?" Cassandra asked.

"Hell yeah, I hit a six-hundred-dollar jackpot on my first pull, soon as I walked thru da doe!"

"You did? What'd Mona do?"

"Sandy, I won a thousand-dollah pot, shidd! I didn't wanna leave, shidd!" Mona bragged.

"OH KAY!" Lorraine said as she gave Mona five, laughing.

"So y'all doin good," Cassandra said.

"Gurll, we whuppin ass."

Lorraine spoke loud enough for the whole bus to hear. Big winners always let it be known. Rainbow sat amused by it all because he knew if he won big, he damn sure wasn't gonna tell it.

The bus rolled up in front of the Sundowner Casino, where a courtesy clerk boarded passing out room keys, instructions, and thirteen-dollar redemption tickets. For many, this would be the only money they had for the remainder of the day. The free chili cheese dog tickets would be dinner, and nickel slots would be their game.

Rainbow carried their luggage to the room, then sprawled out on the bed.

"Baby, what you doin?" Cassandra demanded.

"I'ma take a nap."

"A nap? Rainbow, let's go cash in these coupons."

"Here, you take mine and this hundred. I'll be right here."

Rainbow undressed and went to bed as Cassandra gave him a kiss then headed out the door. Two hours later she returned broke. Rainbow was in the midst of a peaceful sleep and had been farting off the chili beans, so Cassandra cracked the window before stripping down and joining him.

They had sex but her mind really wasn't on it—it was on money. More specifically, she was figuring out how she would get some from her man. This time she would just play it by ear. Rainbow had already begun making comments to her about bingo and lottery playing, so she damn sure wasn't gonna have him talking about slot machines too.

He lay awake deep in thought, wondering if they had committed too soon. Cassandra's lovemaking was A-1, she had a tight frame, cool personality, sense of humor, and the girl was phine, but once they moved in together, he began noticing things that he felt would prevent their relationship from being successful.

She spent too much on frivolous items like fake hair, fake nails, and fake contacts. Constantly perpetrating a fraud, she tried to give off the impression that she had money, when she didn't have shit. His stock was falling fast and he knew it, but he loved her.

"What you want for dinner, baby?" Rainbow asked.

"I'ont know, what you want?"

"Steak and lobster sounds good."

"Steak and lobster—who can afford that?" Her question was serious.

"We can. What, you don't have *any money*?"

"Yes, I have money," she lied, "but I don't want to spend it all on dinner."

"Now since when do you pay for our dinner?" he smirked.

"OK, steak and lobster it is," she conceded with a smile.

"Good, let's get dressed and go to the Eldorado. They sell it for nine ninety-nine."

After showering, they decided to wear their matching black outfits, which consisted of identical slacks, turtleneck sweaters, and kicks. Exiting the room, they held hands while strolling to the elevator. Once outside, they walked one block to the Eldorado Casino.

Inside, Rainbow hugged Cassandra to the counter and ordered steak and lobster meals. They ate, drank a few shots, and Cassandra even played Keno. Rainbow pulled out a pocket camera and asked the neighboring couple to take their flicks, which they did.

Wandering over to the race and sports book section, he checked his bets. All three of his early wagers covered the spread, so they walked to Cal Neva with collection on their mind.

The fifty-dollar bet on three picks paid him three hundred dollars, which he gave to Cassandra minus the original fifty. On his heavyweight college card, all of the first-half scores were routs, but the second half would decide the outcome. That's when the favorites would insert second- and third-string players against the other teams' starters. The bench players would usually turn the game into a scrub match, resulting in numerous turnovers and miscues.

Many coaches would also get conservative in their attack, not wanting to be accused of running up the score against a clearly demoralized foe. Purchasing five two-dollar packs of nickels, Rainbow told his woman, "Baby, let's go play some slots."

"I'm with you, babes," she cheesed.

"I like to play at Circus Circus."

"Let's go," she said.

They walked hand in hand, heading down Virginia Street.

"Dinner was delicious," she stated.

"Yeah, it was, wasn't it?"

"I have a feeling my luck is about to change."

"Oh, you do?" he grinned.

"I sho do, baby—ya better believe it!"

"Well, that remains to be seen."

The streets were filled with people moving about. Some faces were happy while others had "the look," which was the label Nevadans gave those who'd lost their money.

It was the eyes—you could see despair or desperation in them. If your pockets were low, it was written all over your face.

Entering Circus Circus, Rainbow and Cassandra strolled to the gaming area. Rainbow chose a spot at the nickel machines while Cassandra marched off to the dollar slots on the next aisle. Twenty minutes later she returned carrying three one-hundred-dollar trays of coins.

"You won?" He was genuinely surprised.

"I told you my luck would change," she bragged.

"OK, let's go cash out," he said.

"I'm with you, babes." She was giddy.

They marched to the redemption window and cashed out. She still had two hundred of what he'd given her along with the three she'd just won. Cassandra was proud of herself. Rainbow suggested they go to the race and sports book area to check his scores, which they did.

His heavyweight selections all covered the spread.

"Let's go get my scrill," he stated.

"How much you win this time?"

"Five hundred."

"Baby, you doin good! I'ma hafta learn that game—it be payin!"

Rainbow could only smile.

As they left the casino, Cassandra spotted Lorraine and Mona. They were at the nickel machines and had "the look."

"Baby, there go Lorraine and Mona, let's see what they doin."

Cassandra was already making her way to them as she spoke. Rainbow followed.

"Lorraine, Mona, how yaw doin?"

"Girl, we jus killin time," Lorraine lied.

"Me an my man tearin dey ass UP!" Cassandra screamed.

"Yaw is?"

"Sho is. I won a five-hundred dollar jackpot but gave about one seventy-five back, and Rainbow done won eight hundred bettin on football."

"He did?" They said in unison.

"Shit yeah, he fixin ta show me dat game, shidd. OH KAY. Well, ah see yaw tamorrow."

"What are yaw fittin ta do?" Lorraine asked.

"We goin back ta Cal Neva so mah man can collect, then he gone show me how ta do that shit."

"Can he show us too?" Lorraine begged.

"Yeah gurll, let's go."

They all made their way to the door with Rainbow trailing. He really didn't want Lorraine anywhere around him because she was too phine. The longer she was in their company, the more he would look at her frame, and that spelled trouble.

The day had been warm but the cool October night air was brisk, so Rainbow suggested they catch a cab. Besides, his dogs were hurting from being on them the last thirty-six hours. Rainbow helped the women inside the mini-van taxi, with Lorraine being last. He grabbed her hand to assist her when she "slipped." To stop her from falling, one hand grabbed her waist while the other rested squarely on her ass.

Cassandra was turning around in her seat instead of sliding in, so she wasn't aware of it, but Rainbow knew Lorraine had "slipped" on purpose. Still, his manhood stiffened immediately. Lorraine crotch-watched his bone and upon seeing the print, licked her lips as he sat down.

Paying the cabbie, Rainbow took the girls to the sports book and picked up a handful of cards, giving two to each lady. For emphasis, he went to the counter and cashed in his ticket, explaining to everyone that he'd only bet twenty but would win five hundred.

Lorraine and Mona were impressed, eager to learn. Cassandra was a bit more eager this time, too. Rainbow explained the betting scheme, over/under, college, pro, the point spread, everything that came to mind.

"So Rainbow? Who you takin?" Lorraine inquired while smacking gum.

"I already got 'em."

"And who is that?" She was syrupy.

"I got Dallas, Green Bay, and Buffalo for a hundred."

"So if they cover the spread, you win six hundred?" She understood.

"Exactly," Rainbow stated. The girl had game—he was impressed.

"Well, I like Dallas over my Raiders this year.

"Why?" he interrupted.

"'Cause dey don't know what dey doin, that eight and two record is a fluke."

"How can you say that?" he asked.

Cassandra was beginning to get upset because Rainbow and Lorraine were dominating the conversation. She could do nothing to stop it because she didn't understand gaming the way her friend did.

"Well, here, *Rainbow*," Cassandra said, handing him a fifty. "Play that on whatever you pick. We goin to the slots. Y'all ready?" She turned to Lorraine and Mona.

"Gurll, nawww!" Lorraine answered back. "This sounds too easy, and I like football too!"

"Well, ah see ya later then."

"Girl, we'll be there in a minute," Lorraine said.

Cassandra handed Rainbow her fifty, then Mona did the same. Lorraine elected to stay and learn more about the game. Cassandra just assumed she didn't have any more money. She walked with Mona through the casino, then spoke.

"Mona, let's go to another casino. I don't like these slots."

"How 'bout Harrah's?" Mona suggested.

"That'll work, it's right across the street."

Rainbow and Lorraine resumed talking football the minute Cassandra and Mona walked away.

"So why you say the Cowboys gonna beat the Raiders?" Rainbow squinched his face.

"'Cause the Raiders shuffle in too many running backs, defense is weak, and *I* even know what play they gone do!!" Lorraine was emphatic.

"So you know Dallas gone win, huh?"

"I just don't know by how much, but it will be by more than seven," she spoke again with conviction.

Rainbow and Lorraine discussed several matchups and who they favored. She was extremely knowledgeable about sports, telling him that she was an only girl with four brothers, and she learned from them.

They made their bets, with Rainbow paying for his and hers. Cassandra was right; Lorraine was broke. For the next half hour they searched the casino for Mona and Cassandra but could not find them. By now the conversation had turned to likes, dislikes, fears, and triumphs.

Rainbow no longer thought she was hot in the ass, just confused.

"They're not in here," he concluded.

"I know. They must be in Harrah's," Lorraine answered.

"How do you know that?" Rainbow returned.

"Because that's Mona's favorite club."

"OK, let's go there."

They walked across the street and went inside Harrah's. Spotting Cassandra and Mona at the dollar slots, they joined them.

"Hey gurlll," Lorraine spoke to Cassandra.

"Hey back," Cassandra responded dryly.

"We made the bets," Rainbow said as he handed over their tickets.

"Thank you," Cassandra said as she snatched the tickets. "You ready to go to the room?"

"Yes, baby, let's call it a day."

Cassandra and Rainbow walked out of the casino, with her starting in on him as soon as they were out of Lorraine and Mona's eyesight.

"So you like that bitch, huh?" she snarled.

"What bitch?"

"That bitch you been with the last hour and a half! You know what bitch I'm talkin 'bout, Rainbow—don't even go there!" She was angry.

"Cassandra, you left!"

"Then you should'a left."

"Why would I leave when I'm making my bets?"

"Hell, you could'a made yo bets anywhere—you damn sho found the scores in every damn casino."

They took a shortcut through the El Dorado with Cassandra talking so loud now that she was creating a scene. Rainbow felt like hiding under a rock. Other couples were arguing but it was about money, so people didn't care. Their argument was about sex, and that sells.

"Look baby—maybe you could lower your voice?" he reasoned.

"For what? You got something ta hide?" she shouted.

They walked out of the El Dorado with security trailing them. They were bad for business. Since their room at the Sundowner was in the tower, not above the main casino, Rainbow took the back way.

"Rainbow, hey, if you want her, you can have her."

"Want who, baby?"

"LO-rraine, that's who!"

"Baby, I don't want her. You're all I need."

"Rainbow, you mean that?"

"Yes, baby, I mean it."

"I love you, 'Bo."

"I love you too, 'San."

Just like the weather, Cassandra changed. Once again she loved her man. Rainbow shook his head and went to their room. The longer their relationship lasted, the more he noticed this unpredictable flaw in her character.

7

THE PERFECT
GETAWAY

The past three days spent with her new man had been the best of her life. Vanessa could not recall a more satisfying getaway. They had driven to a bed and breakfast inn located in the wine country.

Napa Valley provided a splendid change of pace from the daily grind of the ghetto streets. With rolling hills and lush greenery, the setting was serene. The drive was remarkably traffic-free, with the car radio booming out hit after hit.

To reach the Country Inn you had to drive up a winding two-lane road. The view was breathtaking, with row after row of fruit trees providing what Vanessa thought would make a picturesque postcard scene. As they climbed higher, neatly manicured grass began replacing the orchard. An occasional tree sat alone in an open field surrounded by lawn. Horses and cows roamed, freely eating whatever they desired.

The inn was perched atop the mountain and resembled a slave home. Painted white with blue trim, it had a wraparound porch along with sitting chairs. A flower garden sat off to the side displaying roses, orchids, petunias, and gardenias, along with a hand-crafted sign instructing visitors to park in the back.

The owners were a middle-aged couple who really seemed to enjoy running the place. Aaron Broadhurst was six feet tall with thinning blond hair, piercing blue eyes, rugged skin, and a powerful build. His wife Nancy was short with a Jamie Lee Curtis hair style, dark black eyes, big breasts, small waist, and a nice-looking butt.

They both were perfectionists so they always went above and beyond to make sure their guests were pampered. The inn was filled with beautiful antiques, along with more practical furniture shellacked and varnished to a shine. Any question or concern was treated by the Broadhursts as a major problem and addressed immediately.

Aaron didn't talk much, but Nancy's mouth ran nonstop. They were both dressed in blue Levis, checkerboard shirts, and tan work boots. This, Vanessa would figure out, was their daily attire.

The first evening was spent with Big Ed taking Vanessa's body. His battering ram plowed into her long into the night. By the time he finally dozed off, her heart and soul belonged to him.

It was so quiet, Vanessa could hear crickets chirping outside throughout the night. She slept peacefully, dreaming of how sweet it would be spending her life with her new man. Alvin was a distant memory already. Friday morning they awoke around eleven to breakfast in bed.

She wolfed down her ham, eggs, toast, hash browns, and juice just as voraciously as he did.

After showering together then getting dressed, they cut out. Big Ed scooped up the tourist maps outlining points of interest from the end table, turned off the lamp, and closed the door.

There was a picnic basket sitting outside their door that Big Ed picked up casually and handed to Vanessa. Driving to many of the tourist spots on the map, they saw the sights and displayed loving affection to anyone around.

They ate dinner at a nice seafood restaurant in Petaluma. Stuffed and satisfied with the excellent service, they headed back to their weekend home. Pulling up to the inn just as the sun was beginning to set, Big Ed took Vanessa by the hand and walked to a hilltop. Gazing at the stars he got serious.

"Baby, I love you already and I know you're the only one for me," he said as a wide smile creased her face.

"I love you too, but what about Shirley?" she asked.

Big Ed pulled her into his arms and kissed her passionately. Vanessa's body melted into his as she eagerly kissed him back.

"All I want is you. I just want you to understand that for us to be together one hundred percent, it will take some time."

"OK," she said, loving the feel of his manhood pressing on her belly.

"Just be down for me, dig?"

"Yes baby, I'm down."

Big Ed led her by the hand back to the inn, where Aaron and Nancy sat on the porch.

"Hey you guys!" Nancy greeted "Did you enjoy your day?"

"Very much so," Vanessa answered. "Thank you so much for the basket."

"Honey, no thanks needed, just promise me you'll be back."

"You have my word."

Aaron rose from his seat to walk down the trail with Big Ed, while Vanessa and Nancy engaged in small talk. When they returned, Ed took Vanessa's hand and went to their room. He spent the night giving her the best loving she'd ever received.

Vanessa slept like a baby, waking on Saturday with a serious appetite. One thing about being with Ed she noticed: after fucking him, she wanted food. Nancy had prepared another fabulous breakfast, which they ate in bed.

Showering together, Big Ed bent Vanessa over, taking her body as the water streamed down her back. They took turns soaping down each other, dressed, then bounced.

They first visited a winery in Napa Valley, sampling a few types along with the complimentary cheese and crackers. Lining the walls of the tourist shop were exotic long-neck bottles filled with salad dressings. Next to that were jars of assorted pasta sauces, olives, peppers, and hot wing dips ranging from mild to super hot. They also sold caps, t-shirts, bath oils, cutting boards, corkscrews, cheese, crackers, and pasta. Vanessa purchased two bottles of wine and a corkscrew.

Big Ed asked the man behind the counter if he had any more cheese and cracker trays to put out. The guy told him no, because the "grazers" were having a field day. He went on to explain that grazers were the people who would drink free samples, eat up all the snacks, then leave without spending a dime.

Feeling good, Big Ed and Vanessa drove to the small town of Sonoma, where they picked out a cafe for lunch. Downtown reminded you of a quaint rustic setting from an old western movie. The entire area was a tourist attraction saturated with specialty shops. Parking was free, and there was a landscaped public square in the center of it all where kids could play.

They chose to dine at the restaurant for a five-room hotel in the middle of the block. Sitting outside on the patio, they engaged in lighthearted conversation while waiting for their meals. Vanessa noticed all the stares directed at Big Ed by other patrons.

"Baby, do you notice all these people looking at you?" she asked.

"That always happens."

"It does?"

"Yeah, they thank ahm a football playa."

"Why would they assume that?"

"'Cause I'm big, black, dressed nice, got a chiseled frame, and a model in my company."

"Oh, so you think I have model potential?"

"Gurll, you know you phine, shidd!" They both laughed.

By the time they completed their lunch, Big Ed had Vanessa carrying on as if she were royalty. She seemed to get a kick out of white people staring and gawking at her man. Vanessa nibbled at her spinach salad while Big Ed devoured his steak. After eating they visited every store on the three-block, U-shaped strip before heading back to the inn.

Big Ed maneuvered there deftly even though it was getting dark. Somehow Vanessa knew he'd done this number before. Not because he didn't need the map—it was mainly the way the Broadhurst couple treated him at the boarding house. They stumbled over each other trying to keep him happy.

If she didn't know better, she would have sworn that the entire excursion was paid for with drugs; they may have even been his connection. How else could he get the best room in the house without a reservation? She didn't really care because she knew that when you're in the life, you get those types of privileges.

Nancy had prepared lasagna, tossed salad, and French bread with garlic spread for dinner. The other three couples were seated and conversing when Vanessa and Big Ed walked through the front door. Aaron was placing logs in the fireplace.

"Eddie, looks like you two had a nice day," Aaron said.

"Man, it don't get no better than this." They laughed and shook hands.

"Are you guys having dinner?"

"Aaron, I'm stuffed, but I know your wife will pack me a lunch tomorrow." They laughed again.

"Well, you know Nan won't send you home on an empty stomach. What time will you be checking out?"

"We hope to split early, but you never know." Big Ed eyed Vanessa and smiled, making her blush.

"Well, if I don't see ya, take care of yourself, man."

"You too, Aaron."

"Ms. Vanessa, it's nice to make your acquaintance." Aaron held her hand.

"Likewise Aaron," she responded.

Vanessa and Big Ed trudged up the stairs to their room and closed the door. The minute it shut Nancy came from the kitchen asking Aaron why they weren't eating. She wanted her other guests to meet the black couple.

The room was clean and the linen on the bed fresh. Vanessa felt guilty because she knew Nancy had to notice all the love stains on the sheets. She also knew there would be more waiting tomorrow. While she put away the many items Big Ed had purchased for her, he took a shower.

He returned to the room butt-naked while drying off. Vanessa's eyes focused in on his weapon and subconsciously her hands removed all her clothes. She walked into his arms, then he spoke.

"Take a shower," he whispered as he held her stout frame.

"OK," she said obediently.

"You know we won't be able to go to the game tomorrow, right?"

"I don't care about no game, just you," she giggled.

Vanessa retrieved her overnight bag then headed for the bathroom. She showered, perfumed herself down, toweled off, then strutted out in her birthday suit.

Big Ed sat on the bed with a mirror on his lap. On it was a pile of cocaine powder, which he sniffed liberally. He handed her the tray while stretching, and she took a snort.

Using her index finger to close one nostril while inhaling from the other, she got her high on.

Vanessa pulled out the weed she had in her purse then rolled a joint, sprinkling it with coke. This was called a "gremlin or gremmy" joint, and she loved them. Vanessa was a weed connoisseur, and mixing it with a mind-altering drug was right up her alley. If she didn't have weed, Vanessa would use cigarette tobacco, smoking "caviar joints." Vanessa hit the gremmy and proceeded to make a noise that sounded like a stifled sneeze.

They sat up getting high and drinking wine until midnight. The entire time was spent with Big Ed giving Vanessa his theories on life. Most men call it programming their woman into their way of thinking. Big Ed considered it giving Vanessa free game.

They had sex then fell asleep in each other's arms. Waking up early Sunday morning, Vanessa packed up their belongings and they bounced. When Big Ed opened the room door there was a picnic basket sitting in his path. He picked it up, looked at Vanessa, and they both broke out laughing.

Nancy had packed a snack, as Big Ed knew she would. Once they hit the road Vanessa opened the basket and saw it was filled with cheese, cold cuts, crackers, garlic-stuffed olives, and a bottle of white zinfandel.

The drive home was peaceful and traffic-free until they hit the MacArthur Maze. After the usual twenty-minute logjam, they rolled to the east side. Big Ed maneuvered the Acura into Vanessa's stall and they got out.

Vanessa took out her keys but before she could put

them in the slot, she noticed a business card stuck in the security gate. Lifting it, she froze in her tracks. The card was from a Sargeant Johnson at OPD.

"Baby, it's from the police! How did they find me? What am I going to say?" Vanessa was hysterical.

"Tell 'em you an Al broke up two weeks ago an you ain't seen 'im since," Big Ed stated matter-of-factly as he barged past her into the condo.

Big Ed tossed their athletic bags onto the love seat then sprawled out on the sofa. The minute he dozed, his pager went off. Reaching down, he looked at the number then lifted the phone off the receiver to check his messages. The beeper had been going off all weekend in the wine country, but Big Ed never checked his pages. Vanessa kept her mouth closed every time it went off because she didn't want him upset with her.

The page was from Flea, who wanted to know what to do. Big Ed called him.

"Flea," he boomed, "tell everybody to meet me at da spot in three hours."

"OK boss, anythang else?"

"Naw, jus be dare."

"Das a sheck," Flea slurred.

Big Ed hung up the phone and resumed his nap. Vanessa busied herself putting away their things. She didn't stop to think that Big Ed already had a home. She just happily bagged Alvin's clothes, replacing them with Ed's.

Two hours later Big Ed arose then wandered into the bathroom. He freshened up, then walked out and kissed Vanessa on the mouth. The kiss was long and sensual, arousing the both of them. He wanted to take her right then, but since he had work to do, he strutted out the door.

She locked the door behind him then removed every photo of Alvin. Placing them on the top shelf of her bedroom closet, she picked up the phone and dialed the number on the card.

"Johnson, homicide!" The voice was strong.

"Yes, my name is Vanessa Harris and I found your card in my door."

"Hello, Ms. Harris. I'd like to talk to you about a case I'm working on. Could we meet in an hour?"

"A case?"

"Yes ma'am. I can be at your place in twenty minutes."

"You wanna tell me what this is all about?"

"Yes ma'am, just as soon as we meet. I'm on my way now."

Vanessa hung up the phone and slowly wandered into the living room. She really hadn't grieved for Alvin because she was too busy falling in love. Now resigned to the fact that OPD was on the way with a ton of questions, she surely had to pull herself together.

The twenty-minute wait was over before she could sit down. She turned on her component set, then fed the fish swimming in their tank. The doorbell rang with a loud knock right behind it. Vanessa opened her door.

"Ms. Harris? I'm Sargeant Johnson; this is my partner Sargeant Hernandez." They both displayed their badges.

"Come in," she said as she opened the security gate.

Johnson and Hernandez strode in, with Nathan taking

a seat next to Vanessa at the kitchen table. Manny remained standing.

"Ms. Harris, I need to ask you about Alvin Jenkins," Johnson stated.

"What would you like to know?"

"When was the last time you saw him?"

"About three weeks ago."

"Three weeks?" Nate arched his brow.

"Yes, we had another one of our usual fights so I asked him to leave."

"And you haven't seen him since?"

"No, I haven't."

"So you didn't know he was murdered?"

"Murdered? ... When? ... How?"

"He was slain execution-style Wednesday night, and the body was found Thursday."

After a long moment of silence, Vanessa regained her composure then resumed the conversation. She was playing it off perfectly.

"Where was he killed?" she asked.

"Alvin was murdered at Lookout Point."

"In the hills?" Tears streamed down her eyes.

"Did he have any enemies?"

"No, everybody liked Al," she said.

"Not everybody," Manny blurted in while jotting notes.

"Can you think of anything you can tell me?" Johnson's voice was soothing.

"No, but he did have a few people upset with him because of the game," she whispered.

"Game! Friends Helping Friends?"

"Yes, Alvin talked everyone he knew into investing. Then when it didn't pay off, he had enemies."

"Good! Do you know any of these friends?" Johnson coaxed.

"I know all of 'em, they're all family and folks."

"Folks" were what blacks labeled lifelong associates or close friends.

"Ms. Harris? Could you provide me with a list of names?"

"Yes."

Vanessa sauntered into the bedroom with Manny's eyes greedily following her. She wore white spandex tights with no panties, so all you saw was body. Manny was getting an eyeful. Nate made sure his mini recorder was taping the entire conversation.

"Ms. Harris, do you have any of the old gameboards?" Johnson asked.

"No, I had nothing to do with that scam."

She wrote down a list of names and numbers, then handed them over to Manny.

"Well, I guess that just about wraps it up," Nate said. "If we need any more information, we'll contact you."

"OK."

"Thank you for your assistance."

"You're welcome."

The detectives rose to leave while Vanessa sat dabbing her eyes with tissue. She picked up the phone to call Alvin's mom. Placing it back on the receiver, she decided to wait until her story was straight before facing his folks. Johnson and Hernandez headed for their service vehicle engaged in conversation.

"What do you make of that, Nate?"

"I'm not sure, Manny."

"I think she's lying."

"Why do you say that?"

"Because ... those were not tears of surprise, Nate. They were tears of guilt."

"You're convinced of it?"

"Damn right I'm convinced. She knows something and I intend to find out what."

Nate knew Manny had a point. Matter of fact, he felt the same way. Vanessa Harris was in up to her neck, but it would be hard to prove because she was scared. They cruised off and headed back to the station. Their mission: call Alvin's folks.

GET YO OWN SPOT

Big Ed parked his monster truck across the street from "Da Spot," got out, then headed up the steps, black duffel bag in hand.

Da Spot was an apartment complex located on the east side at 65th and Outlook. It was sky blue with royal-blue trim. A ten-unit two-story building with all the doors facing the same direction, the Golden Eagle apartments were average in appearance.

Situated on the second floor, da spot was the apartment that Big Ed's predecessor Tonio leased for drug sales. Now being the number-one moneymaker themselves, this was the place where the main crew would gather for meetings.

It was a three-bedroom unit, poorly furnished, and run by wannabees. They would usually spend their day's pay, which was always in drugs, on some dopefiend broad, trying to get some snatch.

The house boss was a dude named Skye. He was a rugged Mike Tyson-looking fool. Five foot eight and built like a fireplug, the dude had attitude and build. He ran da spot like the mobster he was—violently.

Skye Barker didn't play and everyone knew it. If an associate's trap was short, a customer "forgot" to pay, or a new dealer attempted to sell on the turf, Skye would personally beat 'em down. He took pleasure in hurting people.

His turf ran from Fruitvale to 82nd Avenue, and da spot was open twenty-four/seven. Customers could always use a room for sex, gambling, or getting high. Of course, Skye would attach a "user fee" for this service, which he'd pocket.

Skye was decked out in a black and gold nylon sweat-suit, complemented by a black Kangol safari brim along with matching sneakers, t-shirt, and white tube socks. He was draped in gold, and when he talked, two gold caps were proudly displayed on his front two teeth.

Next to Skye sat Vinny. He was six feet even on a two-hundred-pound frame. Vinny Neal controlled the area covering 82nd Avenue to the Oaktown/San Leandro border including the hills, which was profitable.

Vinny wore royal-blue slacks with matching Stacy Adams, blue pimp socks, and a blue rayon shirt with red and yellow flowered designs. Like most d-boys, Vinny was saturated in gold. He was cocoa brown with a low-cut afro, lean as a side of beef, long clean-shaven chin, and hand-some. Vinny was also deadly. His weapon of trade was the switchblade, and his skills were impeccable.

On the corner sofa sat Bulldog and Babypit. Bulldog operated out of the Sobrante Park/Brookfield/Dagg neighborhood of Oaktown. His frame was just as the name described. He was solid as a rock, standing five eleven on a powerfully built hundred-and-ninety-five-pound body. Bulldog wore a Lord Jesus hairdo and dressed fly daily, but always out of style. He had a thing for pointed-toe shoes and blazer sport coats, but all in all, he was a fashion disaster. Bulldog was charcoal black and ugly. He didn't bathe regularly so the dude always had an odor. Thinking he was larger than he actually was, Bulldog lived his life like a kingpin, sporting honeys daily with dope or scrill because they gave up a little booty. Big Ed considered him the weak link in the chain because he was a fool with money. . . .

Big Ed also thought Bulldog was a weak link because he was the only one in the organization who didn't have a central location from which to run his business. He ran his turf in front of the neighborhood corner store at 98th and Edes, which Big Ed considered stupid because that made him visible to the Man.

Babypit was the lean-out-the-window man during drive-bys. Once he rose in the ranks, he didn't have to do that job anymore yet continued to do it anyway. The reason why was because he didn't give a damn if he got spotted or shot. His thrill came in blowing fools away and talking shit while doing it. Babypit ran Funktown, the most violent area of the city. This turf assignment was due to the fact that he had the youngest members of the empire on his payroll. Most were teenagers, so they could care less about offing somebody. The juvenile justice system could only incarcerate them until the age of twenty-five. So they knew it didn't matter what sort of felonious crime they committed; they would not be tried as adults in any court of law.

Six-two and a bulky two-twenty, Babypit's physique was rock solid, cascading down from the shoulders to the hips, then expanding downwards to powerfully built legs. Even as a human replica, he was taller than a full-grown pitbull would be, but that was his tag anyway.

Standing were Donnie, Billy Ray, and Flea, who had his usual beer in hand along with keys dangling from the side of his belt loop in classic janitorial fashion.

"Welcome home, Boss—it's good ta see ya," Flea spoke up.

"Listen up, y'all," Big Ed barked before continuing, "we got problems that need immediate attention."

Everyone's focus was glued on Big Ed, so he resumed his rap.

"Shakey Jones is out da pen and thank he a d-boy now. Niggah tryin ta take over cause he got all lat dope his lil brutha Buckey left behind. Skye? He on yo turf thankin he controllin shit already. What you gone do 'bout it?" Big Ed was direct.

Skye was a fighter at heart, but he wanted no part of Shakey. Yet he still didn't want to appear afraid in front of his homeys.

"Man, ah would'a fucked 'im up two days ago, but you wadn't heah," Skye boasted, reputation intact.

Everyone in the room cast quick "yeah right" looks at

each other. They knew that they wouldn't want Shakey
Jones muscling in on their turf, or the ensuing turf war
that would surely follow.

"Alright, we gone roll up on 'im soon as da meetin's
over," Big Ed said. "Vinny? Handlin business as usual!
Bulldog . . . yo shit is raggly. Man, yo trap been bein shoat
regularly. Yet ah'm sposed ta thank it's 'cause of da po
neighorhood you work in? . . . Hell, po folks spend da most.
Get dat shit together, dude." There was no doubt what
Big Ed meant.

"Babypit? Dey tell me yo boy Silky Johnson should be
runnin da turf instead of you, cause he do a bettah job."

"Silky ain't sposed ta be runnin shit—he works fa me!"
Babypit shouted while striking his chest.

"Anyway, dat's da word on da street. Heah." He tossed
the duffel bag to the middle of the room.

His boys all began pulling out wads of cash, handing
them over to Ed and getting their allotment of dope. Each
person's bag had his name written on it with a black marker.
Once they'd sorted out the packages, Big Ed spoke.

"Let's bounce!"

Each man put his goodies into the trunk of his car while
loading up their artillery. Hopping in Big Ed's monster
truck, they went looking for Shakey. It didn't take long
because Shakey was about to cross the street from the
convenience market on MacArthur.

Big Ed screeched to a halt at Shakey's feet, then they
all got out. Flea, Vinny, and the gruesome twosome rolled
up a second later in the Fleetwood, got out, and joined
their crew.

People began scattering, knowing the shit was about to hit the fan.

"Big Ed, whatup dawg?" Shakey said casually.

"Shake, you know dis mah turf and you ain't welcome," Ed boomed.

"Man, dis America, Jack, an last time ah heard, it was still a free country. Whatup Skye? Vinny? Bulldog? Babypit?"

"Look heah, niggah, ah'm givin you only one woanin— you sell on mah turf, you buy from me!"

"An if ah don't?" Shakey was defiant.

"If you don't, yo ass is grass."

Shakey and Big Ed stood face to face while everyone else watched. It wasn't often that two heavyweights squared off like this with the tension so thick you could cut it with a knife.

"Man, ah done woaned you. Dis ain't no game!"

"Look, Ed, fuck you an all you represent, niggah. You muthafuckas ain't fuckin wit no amateur. I ain't goin no goddamn where. Dis 'bout ta be mah goddamn co'nah, anyway."

"Awight fool, you had yo chance."

Big Ed got back in the truck with his henchmen following closely behind. Shakey strode across the street and resumed his kingpin spot. He was upset because none of the fools he had grinding for him stood by his side when danger loomed. Suddenly Nadine paged the beeper she had bought for him the day before. Shakey called her on the cell phone she'd given him.

"Baby, I got lonely, so I called to see if you were almost through." It was more a plea than a question.

"Nadine, you cain't be checkin on me like dat—ahm handlin mah bidness!"

"I know, I just don't want you to get back in trouble."

"TROUBLE!" he shouted, "trouble is you callin me axin what ahm doin—das da only damn trouble ah see! Now take yo ass ta bed and wait till ah get dare!!"

"OK," she said and hung up the phone feeling stupid.

Shakey angrily fished Sheila's number out of his pocket then dialed, unaware that the number would reflect on the next bill they mailed Nadine.

"Hello?"

"Hey gurll."

"Shakey?"

"Who else?"

"I waited for you the other day, but you didn't come back in," she said.

"What you doin right now?"

"I wasn't doin anything."

"Look, I ain't doin nothin either, so ah was thankin me an you could kick it."

"That'll be fine."

"OK, ah'm on mah way."

"I'll be here, baby. My number is three-oh-one."

Shakey hung up and jumped in Nadine's ride. Rolling past Mills College, he stopped at the Shell station on High and filled up the tank. Spotting a middle-aged white woman at the next pump, he began his usual pastime.

"Hey baby, you ain't got ta pump no gas!" he shouted.

"Oh, I don't? she returned.

"Hell naw, I'll do it fo ya."

In the blink of an eye, Shakey took the nozzle from her and began filling up her tank.

"See, if ah was yo man, you wouldn't have ta do this. What's yo name, gurll?"

"My name is Monica, what's yours?"

"Calvin, but you can call me Shakey."

"Why should I call you that?"

"'Cause everybody knows salt and pepper are staple ingredients to any good meal, and once you sample my menu, you won't want nothin else!"

"Is that right?" She was laughing.

"You know it is—now how 'bout you givin me yo number?"

"You give me yours," she said as she played with her wedding ring.

Shakey wrote down his pager number and handed it to her. Returning the nozzle to the pump, he got in the car and rolled down the window.

"Call me when you get hungry, baby."

"OK," she said.

Pulling off, he took 580 to the west side smiling. Monica threw his number in the trash and drove off.

DIS AIN'T NO GAME

Rainbow and Cassandra spent the night making passionate love. He rose early, showered, dressed, and left to go buy coffee, along with the Reno and Oaktown newspapers.

When he returned, Cassandra had showered, packed, and was ready to go. Today they wore matching burgundy sweatsuits. Getting on the bus, Rainbow felt sorry for all the grim faces. Most of the people looked tired, hungover, and broke.

The bus rolled off, heading for the city of Sparks, which is Reno's next-door neighbor. The driver parked in front of Harrah's then went in to fetch an employee. They returned and the service rep began dishing out ten-dollar redemption coupons to each individual, along with the usual discount books.

Cassandra greeted Lorraine and Mona icily, paying no attention to them during the five-minute ride. They knew she was jealous but couldn't understand why, since she was the one who chose to play slots instead of being with her man.

As everyone marched to the redemption center, Lorraine touched Cassandra's arm.

"Girl, we need to talk."

"OK," Cassandra said dryly.

They went to the ladies' room.

"Sandy, look, I don't know why you givin me the cold shoulder, but I just wanted to say if I've done anything to you, I'm sorry."

"Girl, you ain't done nothin, I'm just exhausted," Cassandra lied.

"All yo man did was show me the parley, with yo approval, then I jus feel like you got mad."

"Lorraine, that ain't even it, I'm just tired and ready ta go."

"OK, but you know if you have a problem with me, we can always talk it out."

"I know. I'm glad we cleared the air."

They walked back out and joined Rainbow and Mona in line. Cassandra was happy, talking a mile a minute. Once again Rainbow noticed that she could change like the weather.

The foursome redeemed their coupons for ten dollars each and headed for breakfast. Everyone got nickels except Cassandra, who got bo-dollars, which surprised no one. Cassandra signed the waiting list sheet then was told by the maitre d' that there would be an hour-long wait.

"Well, since we have an hour to kill, we may as well

gamble," she told her man.

"Alright baby, I'm playing nickel slots," he shot back.

"Nickels don't pay shit," she said.

"I know, but it will pass the time away."

"Rainbow, what about our bets?" Mona asked.

"We have to wait until one o'clock to see if we won," he answered.

"Why?"

"Because all three bets we made are ten o'clock games, which won't pay off until one, when the games are over. That's assuming we win."

"So that means since the bus leaves at two, we'll only have one hour to go to Reno, collect, then come back for the bus?" Lorraine chimed in.

"Yeah, so what you do is catch a cab to Cal Neva, get paid, then cab it back here." Rainbow never looked at Lorraine while explaining.

They all took off in different directions. Lorraine and Mona went to the nickel slots, Cassandra to dollars, and Rainbow to watch football. Once the morning games got to halftime, Rainbow headed for the restaurant. The ladies were already there eating.

The waitress took his order and poured him a cup of coffee. He noticed his woman had "the look."

"How we doin, babes?" Cassandra asked.

"Well, Buffalo is in a rout. Green Bay and San Francisco, close, but the Packers have momentum, and the Raiders/Dallas is too close to call."

All Rainbow saw were gloomy looks on their faces after hearing his update. His food arrived and he ate quickly.

They sat people-watching, talking about work and the people they work with, basically killing time since none of them had money except Rainbow.

Cassandra parked her behind at a nickel slot machine looking bored as hell while pulling the one-armed bandit. Mona and Lorraine sat on a bench near the door with the rest of the broke players. Rainbow went back downstairs to watch football.

He returned at one o'clock with a facial expression that showed no signs of being a winner. By now Cassandra had joined her co-workers on the broke bench.

"Let's go!" he stated matter-of-factly.

"We won?" Cassandra looked surprised.

"Yes."

They all jumped up and hugged him, which made him proud. Hopping into a cab, they went to Reno, got paid, then came back to Sparks with attitude. Rainbow had cleared six hundred, all the ladies three.

Since they still had thirty minutes until the bus arrived, Cassandra headed to the dollar slots. Lorraine and Mona followed, while Rainbow went to eat lunch. The women were impressed by the way he could be around all this gambling but not participate.

By the time he joined them on the bus, Cassandra had the look. Lorraine and Mona were full of laughter, meaning they had money. Lorraine had won a five-hundred-dollar jackpot, and Mona had increased her bank by three.

The bus rolled onto I-80, heading home. They played *Let's Do It Again* on the movie screen and Cassandra fell asleep. Lorraine slipped Rainbow two hundred-dollar bills and whispered "Thank You" to him. He pocketed the money and dozed off.

Rainbow awoke as the bus rolled off the freeway and hit MacArthur, passing Mills College. Cassandra was still asleep; so were Lorraine and Mona. He peered around the dark and silent bus until his eyes rested on Lorraine. She slept in a fetal position with her head and upper body covered by her jacket. Her skirt was hiked up, exposing beautiful legs with heels fitting snugly into the imprint lines her behind made.

Rainbow exited the bus and joined the crowd of people jockeying for position to retrieve their luggage. As he and Cassandra went to the car, he dropped his keys. Bending over to pick them up, he fell down and his face slammed violently into the ground.

Cassandra ran over to see what was wrong and why he didn't get up. Slightly turning him, she saw that the skin above his left eye had peeled, displaying blood and dirt. As she turned him more, the realization dawned that he'd been shot.

The bullet shattered his cheekbone, just missing his temple. One inch higher and Rainbow would have been dead. Cassandra screamed for help then called Emergency on her cell phone.

Lorraine and Mona ran over, taking off their jackets and laying them on top of Rainbow's prone body. Cassandra was crouched over him, gently rubbing the back of his neck.

Paramedics arrived, along with the police and fire department. Beat officers began roping off sections of the parking lot as the crowd of onlookers swelled. The EMTs took every precaution to carefully place his body on the gurney and secure him inside the van.

Cassandra gave Mona the car keys and hopped in back of the van. Lorraine trailed in her own car with Mona following closely behind in Bertha. The all sped off to Highland Hospital.

Highland is located in an area of the city known as "Funktown." The unofficial neighborhood logo is a balled-up fist with the index and pinky fingers extended. Surrounded like a triangle by 14th, East 31st, and Vallecita Street, this medical facility is Alameda County's number-one trauma center.

Its appearance on 14th Avenue tends to resemble a haunted house, especially on cold rainy winter nights. An old iron fence spans the three-block stretch, with tree branches hanging over it so low they almost sit on top of cars. The six-story mental ward looms right behind the trees, and since the entire strip is poorly lit, it presents the perfect location for a mugging.

On the Vallecita side an employee parking lot along with outpatient services provide daily doses of methadone for heroin addicts.

East 31st was where you go for public and emergency parking. It's also the main entrance to the hospital.

The ambulance's siren screamed as the vehicle pulled into the parking lot. Mona and Lorraine parked in the stalls designated "Emergency Only." The EMTs jumped out and rolled the stretcher through the sliding doors.

Cassandra and her friends followed closely. Once inside

they frowned at all the people on stretchers lining the hallway. She went to the counter and began giving the attendant information on Rainbow. Lorraine and Mona stood behind her, rubbing her back, shoulders, and neck.

Meanwhile her man was swiftly rolled into the operating room. Cassandra didn't have all the necessary information, but she did know that Kaiser was his regular hospital. The triage nurse reassured her that Kaiser would fill in the blanks, and as soon as he was well enough, he would be transferred there.

They took seats in the waiting area before Cassandra realized that she hadn't informed Rainbow's family of the shooting. Taking her cell phone from her purse, she called his mother.

"Hello."

"Hi, Miss Pearlie Mae, it's me, Cassandra."

"Hey baby, how yaw doin?"

"We just got back from Reno."

"What yaw win?"

"Miss Pearlie Mae, Rainbow's been shot!"

After a long pause, Pearlie Mae spoke: "Where yaw at, baby?"

"At Highland. Rainbow's in surgery."

"We on our way."

The phone line went dead, so Cassandra pushed the "end" button on her cellular. She hung up feeling like the weight of the world was on her shoulders. Glancing around the waiting room, she became even more depressed. The county hospital serviced anybody with Medi-Cal, so you saw some of the strangest characters around. People were filthy, stinking, and mentally unstable. The waiting room chairs were so dirty that you almost believed they were meant to be that color, until closer inspection revealed otherwise.

"Cassandra, what happened?" Rochelle hollered as she stormed into the room with Pearlie Mae following.

"We was getting off the bus, gettin our luggage, then all of a sudden, Rainbow fell down and wouldn't get up. As I turned him over, I realized he was shot, so we came here."

"Well, yaw know who did it?" Pearlie Mae demanded as she stood with her hands on her hips. Pearlie Mae was Rainbow's mother. A frail woman, she wore blue polyester slacks, white tennis shoes, and a blue ruffled blouse with black oversized puff jacket. Her hair was pulled back into a bun and her face displayed a pained expression. Her oak-complexioned skin, deep-set eyes, thin face, and dimple in the chin were all wet with tears.

Pearlie Mae had spent her life using the welfare system, like so many others. This caused her to be timid whenever she felt authority was present—usually in places such as hospitals, offices, and police stations. She was considered an angel in the hood because she treated everyone as a human being, no matter what cruel hand they were dealt in life. However, in an environment such as this, she was out of her league.

Lorraine and Mona sat on each side of Cassandra, consoling her, while Pearlie Mae searched for an available seat. Rochelle stalked off towards the nurse's station. There she would put on a show for the entire waiting room to see.

Rochelle was Rainbow's younger sister, but the similarities ended there. A welfare client her entire adult life, she'd given birth to five children by three different losers. Big as a house, she had no problem fist-fighting men or talking crap. Feeling as if the world owed her something, she viewed her monthly AFDC checks as her well-deserved money. Her mentality was stuck on stupid and she was greedy. Her brain was already calculating how much money would be left if her brother didn't survive, along with what her "cut" would be, being his sister and all.

"Excuse me? I'm trying to find out about Reggie Jordan's condition," Rochelle asked, using Rainbow's given name.

"Mr. Jordan was just admitted, so I don't have any information," the nurse responded.

"No info-mation, NO INFO-MATION!! What da fuck yaw runnin heah wit no goddamn info-mation?" The peanut gallery roared.

"Ma'am, if you'll just have a seat, the doctor will.

"Da doctor, shit! Ah wanna know what's happenin wit mah brutha!" The Night Train liquor was kicking in.

Security appeared out of nowhere, escorting Rochelle to a seat. She joined everyone else while glaring back menacingly at the nurse. The nurse was indifferent, ignoring the first of many fools who would clown at her station tonight.

Lorraine and Mona rose to leave.

"Sandy, if you need anything, call me!"

"OK, Lorraine."

They each gave Cassandra a hug and said goodbye to Pearlie Mae and Rochelle—who were already taking their empty seats—then bounced. Cassandra remained seated with her face buried in her hands.

10
A DEADLY NIGHT

Slack cleaned off the high-powered rifle he used, put it back in its case, then casually walked out of the empty house. He'd found a home on Halliday Street, which sat right behind Bancroft Avenue. Camping out in an upstairs bedroom, he waited. Two hours later he struck pay dirt when Rainbow and Cassandra's party bus eased into the mall.

As Rainbow retrieved their luggage, Slack zoomed in on his temple with his scope. Just when he pulled the trigger, Rainbow bent over. That split second's worth of movement may have saved Rainbow's life, but Slack didn't know it. His report to Shakey would be "mission accomplished."

Slack walked briskly down the block and around the corner to his bucket, which was parked on Church Street. Stopping momentarily, he stuffed the rifle into a container that sat on the street waiting to be picked up the next morning by garbage men.

Heading home to the west side, he stopped for a bottle of T-bird at the convenience market on MacArthur. Shakey sat on a stump in front of Baskin-Robbins watching all activity. Seeing Slack pull up at the store, he crossed the street and waited for him to come out.

"Slack baby, what you doin on my side of town?"

"I was handlin yo bidness."

"Rainbow?"

"Popped dat ass propah," Slack boasted.

"Good shit, man—ah didn't know you was gone do it so soon, dough."

"Why wait?" Slack grinned.

"How much ah owe you, dude?"

"Nuttin! Dat shit was fo Buckey an Violet."

"Man, ah wish ah could'a been dare—why you didn't tell me, fool?"

"You got mo impotant thangs ta do." Slack pointed at the corner and they both broke out in large smiles.

"Yeah, dis shit goin smoove, dawg."

"You rackin up, huh?"

"Slack, dat ain't da word, ah feel like ahm stealing candy from a baby. Dese niggahs be fiendin fa dat shit, man, ghin me everythang dey got." Shakey talked like a kingpin.

"Dig it, das what yo people do."

"Mah people—dey was yowne 'foe mine." They busted up hugging each other.

"Shake, ah gotta go—you know 'Lon gone be worried sick if mah ass don't show up."

146

"Yeah, ah know—what about Sheila, dough?"

"Man, she was upset that you didn't come back, but she sweet on you, homes."

"Niggah, dey all sweet on me: Nadine sweet, Sheila sweet—hell, Cassandra still sweet, bitch jus don't know it." He looked indifferent.

Slack smiled and said, "Dude, I'll call you tomorrow."

"Awight Slack. Tell 'Lon I said whatup."

Slack got in his hoopty and sped off. He felt good because killing folks always got him off. Glancing in his rearview mirror before turning on Seminary, he saw Shakey surrounded by a gang of thugs. Slack made another sharp right into the Chevron service station, killed the engine, and reached for his binoculars.

Peering intently, he spotted Ed Tatum along with his top lieutenant Skye in Shakey's face. Next he saw Ed's Caddy roll up and more henchmen get out. Shakey was outnumbered at least seven to one.

Slack watched as Shakey and Ed stood face to face, obviously disagreeing. Realizing that he'd just tossed his weapon, Slack was nervous because he couldn't help his road dog. Big Ed got back in his ride with his folks following suit. Slack sped up Seminary towards the 580 freeway.

Taking the West Street exit, he headed to Dogtown and Spodie's garage, which is where he kept his heavy artillery. Mama McKnight's bedroom was blue with the television screen, but Slack figured it was probably watching her once again, instead of her watching it.

He went in the garage, locked the door behind him, then headed for his "babies." Slack cherished his weapons in the same manner as any collector would their antiques, beanie babies, or baseball cards—the main difference being that he would dispose of them after each hit, wiping off all fingerprints.

His stash was kept inside a fake wall unit that Slack had personally built. On display were silencers, scopes, assault rifles, handguns, and a couple of hand grenades. Tonight he would use a Glock nine-millimeter, hunting rifle with a scope, and an Uzi just in case war broke out. He took two silencers for the Glock and Uzi.

Carefully checking his guns and oiling the rifle with Three-in-One, he replaced the fake wall and locked the garage, satisfied with his selections. Hopping in his bucket, he headed back to the east side for what he hoped to be a surprise visit with Big Ed and his east-side crew.

Slack rolled up to the corner of 64th and Outlook, parked, then casually walked down the block with his T-bird in hand. To anyone looking, he appeared to be a drunk wandering down the street getting his drink on. What they didn't know was that he was an assassin on his way to a deadly mission, and the bottle of liquor was his prop.

Hiding behind bushes in back of a burned-down apartment building on 65th, Slack waited. The place was right next door to the Golden Eagle, and since it sat higher up on the hill, Slack would be above his prey looking down.

After polishing off his T-bird along with four generic cigarettes, he saw the apartment door open. Customers had come and gone during the past hour buying their poison, but this time someone was coming out.

Bulldog, Babypit, and Vinny walked out and immediately began talking about Big Ed. Bulldog talked while Babypit and Vinny nodded their heads in agreement.

"Man, yaw heah dat muafucka talking 'bout ah bettah get mah shit ta-gether? Shidd, dat niggah bettah leave me da fuck alone!" Bulldog was angry.

"Word up! Fool talkin 'bout Silky sposed ta be runnin mah shit! He bettah worry 'bout Shakey Jones an let me handle mah bidness, shidd!" Babypit growled.

They marched down the steps then headed up the hill to their cars, straight in Slack's direction. They continued to say things about Big Ed behind his back that they would never say to his face, unaware of the set of eyes watching their every move.

Bulldog and Vinny got in their rides and drove off. Babypit opened his trunk to retrieve his dope. Hearing footsteps, he peered over the car, but it was too late. Slack fired. Babypit was dead instantly. His blood splattered over the trunk as his upper body slumped into it. As he began sliding downward, Slack heaved him inside. Before closing it, Slack took his Glock and dope.

Burying his own piece into a hole he'd dug while waiting, he covered it up then patted it down with his feet. Walking briskly down the block, Slack got in his hoopty and cruised off.

The intersection of 90th and MacArthur was filled with activity, as usual. On one corner sat a liquor store with parking for about eight cars. Fools loitered out front, harassing any and everyone. Close by was an empty lot next to the Mission Motel, where dope fiend hookers plied their trade.

Across the street was a small candy store that closed before nightfall, but people stood there anyway, waiting on buses heading south to East 14th or east to San Leandro. The remaining corner had a self-service car wash where idiots would peel rubber pulling out, then do doughnuts into the very large intersection.

Vinny eased his Benz into the car wash, got out, and strode across the street to the liquor store. Happy faces greeted him because everyone knew he had re-copped. Vinny stood signifying for about twenty minutes, which most big-money-having blacks did to people daily. He made a comment or smart remark about anyone who happened to come to the store. Everyone laughed at most of what Vinny said even if it wasn't funny, because he was the man. Once he was done, he motioned for Muggsy and Damon, two of his top associates, to come with him.

They followed him to his car, which was his pride and joy. It was a burgundy 450 SEL with grey leather interior, complete with star wires, vogue tyres, gold lettering and emblems along with bug shield, tinted windows, and silver trim on the skirts.

Moving quickly, Vinny opened the trunk and unwrapped his triple-beam scale, which he placed on the carpeted bed. Next, he calibrated the scale to be sure it would produce an accurate reading. Setting it at a half pound, he watched as the scale's lever dropped, then poured cocaine into a ziplock bag until it rose back to the center.

He repeated the task then handed each man their package in return for the five thousand dollars they gave him. The entire transaction took less than two minutes, yet they all were still nervous.

There was a bum in dirty coveralls and a golf cap searching for cans and bottles in the trash receptacles, but none of the men considered him a threat. He apparently just wanted to get a head start on tomorrow's whiskey money. What they were afraid of was Five-O or some dope fiend who had robbery on his mind.

Since the deal went off without a hitch, everyone was relieved. Muggsy and Damon walked back to the store, got in their rides, and drove off, waving at Vinny, who closed his trunk and got in his Benz. The store's lot cleared, with everyone following either Muggsy or Damon to their spots. Dope would certainly be plentiful tonight.

Vinny looked up to see the bum at his door holding a spray bottle and rag.

"What you wont, fool? Ah don't need mah windows did!" Vinny shouted.

"Who said anythang 'bout windows?"

Slack raised Babypit's Glock to Vinny's eyes, which became big as saucers upon seeing the gun. Before he could plead for his life, he was dead. Shit poured out his body, ruining the car's interior and his trousers as Slack shot him in the heart, then for good measure, fired three more times.

Vinny fell over in the seat as Slack took off the silencer then dropped the weapon in his lap. He wanted it to appear to Five-O that Babypit and Vinny were at war with each other. Knowing Johnson and Hernandez like he did, he knew this would be their conclusion once they traced the gun.

Slack crossed the street and walked down the block towards Castlemont High. He stopped briefly at a body and fender repair shop where he tossed the coveralls, gloves, spray bottle, and golf cap into a trash bin on the side of the building. He always got rid of all incriminating evidence, but since silencers were awfully hard to come by, he did not throw that away. Easing into his bucket, which was parked in front of the East Oakland Health Clinic, he cruised on.

Stopping briefly at the liquor store, Slack bought another bottle of T-bird and a pack of GPCs. Taking a long swig of his juice, he glanced over at the Benz in the car wash stall and grinned. It would be morning before anyone knew what happened, and he would be long gone.

The corner of 98th and Edes was chaotic as usual. At least thirty fools hung out in front of the Rexall drug store doing what street hoods were famous for: being a nuisance. Across the street an even larger knot of knuckleheads loitered in front of the corner market, laundromat, insurance office, and shoeshine stand. Cars zipped by at a rapid pace nonstop.

Whites in their vehicles heading to the airport or freeway, if caught at the light, would be petrified at all the commotion going on. Black men, young and old, drank and got high as if it were legal. They'd bob their heads to music, make lewd gestures to motorists, and sell dope, food stamps, and stolen goods to any buyers.

Bulldog strutted up to the corner and resumed his customary kingpin spot at the shoeshine stand. Taking a seat, he got his pointed toes shined by Mister Ross, a Scatman lookalike who saw and heard nothing. Yet if Bulldog wanted any information, this guy had the answers. A family man, Scatman ran his spot like a professional business. The shoeshine earnings had sent all three of his daughters to college. He was respected by everyone because no one considered him a threat. Since he was almost eighty years old, had two trainees working for him, and could keep a secret, he was glorified.

"Whatup, Scatman?" Bulldog asked as he took a seat.

"Nuttin much, Mistah Bulldog. What'll it be ta-day?"

"Jus shine me up, dawg—da usual."

"OK, Mistah Bulldog."

Slack parked on 99th, got his pool cue bag from the trunk, then headed for the empty field across the street. The weeds in this forsaken, unpaved spot had grown six feet high, and once Slack peeped out the setup, he realized that the spot was unacceptable. There was too much traffic flowing on 98th for him to get off a clean shot.

He could care less about killing some innocent bystander or passenger in a car, but he didn't want Bulldog to have any suspicions that the intended target was him.

Taking a swig from his T-bird bottle, Slack headed for an apartment complex down the block on Edes. Slack climbed the back stairs of a three-story building, stood on the wood railing, then hoisted himself up on the roof. Walking gingerly across, he chose his spot then resumed the mission at hand. Pulling his rifle out of the bag, he assembled it. Carefully placing the scope and silencer on his piece, he crouched over an air duct for support.

Taking dead aim, he fired. The bullet whizzed by Mister Ross' ear and killed Bulldog instantly. It was a direct hit to the forehead. The force of the blow snapped his head back then forward, causing his body to tumble off the chair.

Mister Ross attempted to stop his fall but the effort was futile. Bulldog's head bounced on the pavement, and as Mister Ross screamed for help, people scattered. Slack disassembled the rifle, put the pieces back into his bag, then tip-toed across the roof. Lowering himself quickly, he eased down the steps. Opening the bag, he put parts of the weapon in three different trash bins, then got in his ride and headed home.

Mister Ross was shaken down to the spine from the thought of a bullet that close to his head. The police arrived with their usual questions, but since he knew nothing, they let him go. He began packing up his things because once the police investigation was over, he would never return there to shine shoes. As of tonight, Mister Ross was retired.

Slack drove down Edes to 105th, hooked a left to East 14th, then took 106th until reaching the 580 freeway. After stopping briefly at Spodie's to hide his Uzi, he went home.

Yolanda sat at the kitchen table snapping peas for tomorrow's dinner when her man entered.

"How'd it go?" she asked.

"Like clockwork," he smiled.

Slack gave her a peck on the lips, then sat down at the table while she rose and began fixing his meal. Because he was so skinny, you never would guess that he ate enough for a man twice his size. Tonight he would dine on teriyaki turkey wings, red beans, rice, and hot-water corn bread.

Dinner was prepared, but the kids had devoured all the cornbread before going to bed, so she would have to make more. Yolanda microwaved his plate for four minutes, then turned the burner to high and added cooking oil to her cast-iron skillet. While that got hot, she combined one cup each of corn meal and flour in a bowl and a little salt, plus a heaping tablespoon of sugar. Next, she poured some hot water from the tea kettle into her batter. Taking a wire whisk, she blended the ingredients into a bowl, adding more hot water until the batter was thick and moist.

Turning on the cold water at the faucet, she held her hands beneath it. Satisfied, she dug her hands into the mixture and made patties with the dough, then carefully placed them into the skillet. Once they were golden on the bottom side, Yolanda turned them over with a spatula.

She worked quickly, returning her hands to the cold water before shaping each piece of bread. This action neutralized the heat from the mix. Setting Slack's meal on the table, she washed her dishes, finished cooking her bread, then sat back down to resume snapping peas.

Yolanda knew Slack would not talk about tonight's killings. He never did.

"Shakey's over at Sheila's crib," she stated.

"He is?" Slack was surprised.

"Yes, he got there about an hour ago."

"Mah boy Shake. What you thank about dat?"

"Who? Shake an Sheila Rae?"

"Yes."

"I thank dey might be good for each other." She hoped this to be true.

Yolanda got up and dumped her pea ends into the trash, putting the snapped ones in a bowl of water. Placing them into the refrigerator, she poured him a glass of T-bird. This was the only time he used a glass with his liquor—at home.

Slack polished off his food and drink, then headed for the bathroom to take a shower. By the time he was done, Yolanda had cleaned up the kitchen, turned off the lights, and waited naked in bed.

He closed and locked the bedroom door with a sheepish grin on his face. Over the years along with each child, the frequency of intercourse diminished between these two. But she always gave him some after he committed murder because there was something about death that got him off.

To be a big woman, Yolanda was an excellent lover. She'd let him ride her until he came, then would hump and buck furiously with him holding on for dear life. Slack would resemble a cowboy at the rodeo trying to tame a steer.

By the time she was done, they were both exhausted. Slack rolled over and fell asleep instantly. Yolanda put on her houserobe, went to the bathroom to piss, then joined her man in bed. She slept peacefully that night.

11
PAYBACK

Big Ed walked out of the apartment slapping hands with
Skye.

"Ah scared da shit out dat niggah," Ed stated proudly.
"Shakey don't want none uh mah ass, shidd!"

"Yeah, Boss—niggah tried ta play it off like he was tough,
but you see didn't none of his boys come over dare," Skye
noted.

"I'mo give 'im one mo day, den if he still dare, we gone
put a foot in his ass."

"You ain't said nuttin but a word, Boss."

They were halfway down the stairs before Skye noticed
Babypit's Caddy still parked up the hill.

"Damn, dat don't make no sense," Skye said as he
scratched his head.

"What?" Big Ed asked.

"Babypit's hoopty still dare."

"He probly rode wit one uh dose fools—you know dey all was mad cause ah clowned 'em."

"Ah know, but you'd still thank da niggah would go distribute product." Skye was direct. "See, dat's why ah make da most money, cause ah handle mah bidness."

"Dude, ah see you tamorrow," Big Ed spoke as he shook Skye's hand.

"Awight, Boss."

Big Ed climbed into his monster truck and drove away. Skye headed back towards the building when he thought he saw something hanging from the trunk of Babypit's ride. Going over to get a closer look, he noticed it was a piece of the shirt Babypit wore tonight.

Skye went to his carport, unlocked the trunk of his car, then pulled out a pair of gloves along with a large screwdriver that he would use to pop the trunk if the car was locked. Covering his hands with the gloves, he checked the door. It was unlocked.

Sliding inside the car, he popped the trunk release button, then went to the back to see what was up. What he saw made his stomach turn. Babypit lay inside the trunk dead as a doorknob. Skye closed the trunk, pulled out his cell phone, and called Big Ed.

"Talk ta me," Big Ed said.

"Boss, we got a problem."

"Damn, Skye, ah jus left dare."

"Boss, Babypit's dead!" Skye hollered.

"Dead?"

"Yea, dat niggah layin in da trunk of his ride, dead."

Big Ed pulled over to the curb in his truck, inhaled deeply before exhaling, then spoke.

"How'd it happen?" he asked Skye.

"Boss, somebody shot 'im, then throwed 'im in da trunk."

"Dat muthafuckin Shakey Jones, ah know I'mo kill his ass now!" Big Ed was furious. "Skye?"

"Yeah, Boss?"

"Pop da ignition an drive da car somewhere else, den meet me back at da spot."

Big Ed hung up the receiver before Skye had a chance to answer. He didn't notice because he was too busy heading back to the apartment to get Flea, Billy Ray, and Donnie. They jumped into the Fleetwood while Skye got in Babypit's Coupe de Ville.

Making a U-turn, Big Ed headed back to 65th. He knew it was Shakey, but he didn't think that the fool would strike this quickly. At any rate, this meant war.

Skye jimmied the ignition, then made a left turn and drove Babypit's Caddy to the cemetery on 64th. It covered six city blocks, with grave markers and headstones saturating the landscape. The fact that it was located right across the street from Concordia High and one block from Frick Middle School reminded the children daily that death was real.

Parking on the street, he bailed out and hopped into the car with Flea and the gruesome twosome. They sped back to da spot, where Big Ed was waiting, pacing the floor.

"Ah parked by da cemetery," Skye blurted out.

"Good. Go get yo shit," Big Ed demanded.

Big Ed began loading his Glock with bullets then placed the gun in a shoulder holster. Next, he checked his Derringer before hiding it in an ankle holster. Still not done, he grabbed an AK47 assault rifle and double-checked that.

Reaching into his oversized athletic bag, he pulled out a pair of black Levis, black skull cap, tennis shoes, and cotton turtleneck shirt. These were his killing clothes, which he had not worn since taking over the empire for Tonio.

Skye entered the living room decked out in black jeans, tennis shoes, and a hooded sweatjacket. He was strapped to the max, with nothing but bad intentions on his mind. Billy Ray, Donnie, and Flea sat patiently on the sofa.

"Let's raise! Billy, you drive me. Flea, you roll wit Donnie and Skye," Big Ed ordered.

All five men prepared to leave when another idea struck Big Ed.

"Hold up, y'all—I'mo call Vinny and Bulldog so dey can watch dey back."

Everyone sat back down while the boss dialed Vinny's cell phone number. There was no answer so he called Bulldog.

"Hello?" The voice did not belong to Bulldog, so Big Ed hung up.

"Damn, dass da got-damn police on Dog's phone. Sumthin done happened."

Just as he finished speaking, his cellular rang. The boys were getting restless.

"Talk ta me!"

"Boss, it's me, Lou."

"What's goin on, Lou?"

"Dog's dead."

"How?"

"He got sniped sittin in the shoeshine chair."

"DAMN!" Ed screamed. "Hey Lou, thanks fa da foe-one-one."

"OK, Boss."

"Less go, yaw," Big Ed said.

"What happened to Bulldog?" Flea asked.

"His ass dead too," Big Ed muttered as he stormed out the door.

They got in their rides then rolled to the convenience market, but Shakey was nowhere to be found. Flea pulled up on the right of Billy Ray and rolled down the passenger window. Big Ed looked down and shouted instructions.

"Flea, follow us to dat bitch's house."

Billy Ray sped off to Nadine's crib with Flea on his tail. Big Ed and Billy Ray pulled up right in front of Nadine's building while Flea made a U-turn, parking across the street.

Big Ed strutted up to the door sliding leather gloves on his massive hands. He rang the bell. Nadine, thinking it was Shakey, opened it. This mistake would cost her severely.

Big Ed put his gun up to her temple and grabbed her by the neck with his free hand. Whispering in her ear, he spoke: "Bitch, where he at?"

"Wh ... wh ... where who at?" she stuttered.

Big Ed clamped his hand over her mouth then eased the door shut with his gun hand. Manhandling her from room to room, he searched the entire unit. Realizing that Shakey was not there, Ed released his vice grip from Nadine's mouth, grabbing her neck as a replacement.

"Now ahm only gone ax you dis one mo time—where dat niggah at?"

"Please, I don't know. I think he down the street."

Big Ed squeezed Nadine's neck while slowly lifting her off the floor. Nadine shot her heels up backwards in an attempt to kick him in the nuts, but Ed closed his legs, dropped the gun, then applied a carotid choke hold.

Nadine attempted to scratch his eyeballs, which infuriated Big Ed. He lowered her to the floor, then snapped her neck violently like a pretzel. Piss ran down her leg as she crumpled to the floor in a heap.

Big Ed picked up his gun and walked out the door, locking both it and the security gate. Skye and Donnie stood ready and waiting. The three of them walked back to their rides where Flea and Billy Ray sat with motors running.

"Let's go over dare on High Street where his ex-bitch at!" Big Ed growled.

They hopped in their hooptys and headed for Rainbow's pad in search of Cassandra. If Big Ed couldn't find Shakey, he would send a message to him by killing his women. Unknown to them, Cassandra was at Highland Hospital with her man, who was clinging to his life.

The house was dark so they parked on Rosedale, which was the stem in Agua Vista's T-shaped street. Big Ed and Billy Ray got out, going over to the Fleetwood.

"Donnie, you and Billy Ray go check it out," Big Ed ordered.

The gruesome twosome hurried over to the house and lumbered up the driveway. Donnie reached over the gate to unlock it when he noticed a pair of eyes. Next he heard a growl but before he could react, Iceberg leaped into attack mode.

Donnie pulled his hand away just in the nick of time: one second longer and it would have been bitten off. Iceberg barked loud and continuous as Donnie and his brother ran down the driveway.

Lights from neighboring houses flicked on as they got in the Caddy. Flea hit the accelerator. Big Ed slid into the driver's side of the Bronco and followed. Flea pulled over on High Street.

Big Ed got out and walked over to them.

"What happened?" he asked.

"Niggah got a guard dog," Billy Ray blurted out.

"Why yaw didn't shoot it?"

"Big Ed, we couldn't see da muafucka!" Donnie shot back angrily.

"OK, dis what we gone do. Yaw take Skye back to da spot, den lay low. We'll all meet in da moanin at Skye's place."

They all nodded in agreement, so Big Ed hopped in his monster truck and sped off. Flea reached under the seat, handed each man a beer, lit up a joint, then took back streets to da spot.

Big Ed parked in the driveway of his crib. Getting out, he noticed that sheets had replaced the mini-blinds, and all the lights were on in the home. This was out of character for his wife to be up so late but not unexpected.

They lived on 84th and Olive in a rented three-bedroom home. It was painted beige with brown trim and displayed a neatly manicured lawn. The windows were covered by security bars, as were both the front and back doors. Rent was only one hundred and twenty dollars a month, thanks to Section 8 vouchers. Shirley also received the full complement of government freebies, due to the fact that the welfare system thought she was on her own. They didn't know about Big Ed, and he and Shirley had no intentions of telling them. On her welfare application, children's birth certificates and social security card applications, she always put the father's residence as Los Angeles, claiming that she didn't know his social security number.

The few times she'd been called in for face-to-face meetings with government staff, she played stupid. By the time Shirley got through with the eligibilty workers, they'd think she was a fool. She'd spin up fantastic tales of how lonely it gets sometimes without a man around, and the difficulties of raising two children alone. Their father was married, living with his wife and kids in L.A., but would stop through from time to time with presents.

Shirley Tatum, once upon a time phine, was now big as a house. She perceived her self-esteem to be high because they always had a big bank, but in reality, the girl's self-esteem was as low as it gets.

Hearing the truck pull up in the driveway, she came outside and waited while Big Ed got his things.

"I hope she was good!" his wife hollered.

"You hope who was good?" he replied calmly.

"Dat bitch you been wit da last three days."

"Look, baby, I ain't in no good mood so don't clown 'fo you hear mah story."

"Hey, I'm all ears, buddy."

Big Ed trudged into their home with his athletic bag. Casually locking his guns in a treasure chest in the bedroom, he went into the living room and plopped on the sofa.

Shirley waddled in behind without noticing the look of disgust on his face. She wore a flowered button-down housecoat, run-over slippers, and a scarf on her head. The lumps on her behind produced an ugly picture.

Big Ed wondered to himself how he ever got into this predicament. If it weren't for the children, he'd have left her years ago. She had no education, no job, and no future. He was stuck.

"Well, I'm waiting," she huffed.

"Kids asleep?" he asked quietly.

"Yeah," she snorted.

"What happened when da police came?"

"What you thank? Dey toe up mah goddamn house lookin fa yo ass."

"Look girl, you bettah put a zip on yo lip fo ah do it fa ya."

"You ain't gone do shit! You hit ME and I'll have da police on yo ass so quick, you won't know what hit you. I ain't one uh dose hoes you be fuckin wit, niggah!" She stood with her hands on her hips defiantly.

"Look baby.

"I ain't ya baby—ah thank you just left her, hello!"

"Babypit and Bulldog are dead."

"What?" She didn't believe it.

"Yeah, dey bofe got kilt tonight."

"How?"

"I'ont know, but dey dead. Shakey Jones did it, so you know his ass is good as dead too!"

"Well, I'm sorry to hear 'bout yo friends but hey, that's the life they chose to live."

"You don't give a damn, do you?"

"Hell naw, ah don't give a damn 'cause dat don't explain the rest of dose days you was gone."

"Gurll, ahm a grown man who ain't got ta explain shit!" he hollered.

"Awight den, since it's like dat, I ain't gone be explainin shit ta yo black ass no moe."

Big Ed moved like a track star at the starter's pistol, grabbing Shirley by the neck.

"Let me go!" she demanded through clenched teeth.

"Awight bitch, I'mo let you go, fa good! You sorry fat-ass hoe."

"You da hoe, muthafucka—dass what ah say 'bout yaw Leos, ya Leehoes."

Big Ed went to the room and got his guns while Shirley began her all-out tirade.

"Yeah, probly fitna go back ta da bitch. Mah momma told me ah never should'a got wit yo ass."

"Aw, yo stanky-ass momma ain't shit, always lookin fa free dope!" he shouted.

"What about yo sorry-ass momma!"

"Look Shirley, let's keep mommas outta dis."

She knew he meant it. "Alright den, jus leave."

Shirley sat down on the sofa while Big Ed calmly packed his bags. As he walked out the door without saying goodbye, she screamed, "Say goodbye ta yo kids, you sorry low-life'd muthafucka!"

Slamming the door, she began to cry. Big Ed got into his monster truck and drove off, heading to Vanessa's crib, where he knew pleasure waited.

THE HEAT IS ON

Johnson and Hernandez reported for their shift on Monday after working all weekend. They hadn't had a day off in three weeks, and fatigue was wearing them out. Today they were immediately greeted by Spitz at the door. Something was up because their boss was in a jovial mood, which was certainly unusual for him.

"Gentlemen, I have both good news and bad," he said while marching them into his office.

"Lay it on us," Johnson said dryly.

"Well, the good news is that my transfer request has been granted. As of next Monday, I'll run Personnel and Training."

"Congratulations, sir," they both said in unison.

"Thanks, guys."

Spitz propped his legs on the desk, crossed them, then cupped his hands and placed them behind his head. Johnson and Hernandez sat down, relieved to finally be free of this fool.

"The bad news is that three murders were committed last night, along with an attempt."

"Any suspects?" Johnson asked.

"Not yet, but the dead were all drug dealers working for the east-side empire."

"And the attempt?"

"A guy you two know well, Rainbow Jordan."

They leaned forward in their chairs. Rainbow had assisted them in solving a case a few months back, and both men considered him a good guy.

"What happened to Rainbow?" Johnson asked.

"A sniper took a shot at him as he departed a bus trip returning from Reno. The bullet shattered his cheekbone and came within inches of his temple, which would have killed him." Spitz spoke matter-of-factly.

"Where is he now?"

"I believe he's at the trauma center."

"Let's go, Manny!" Johnson boomed.

They headed for the door before Spitz could utter another word. He didn't care because in one more week he wouldn't have to deal with these two bull-headed clowns anyway. He reassigned the murder case he had chosen for them to another detective team, then began packing.

Johnson pulled into an emergency parking stall at Highland, then he and his partner marched through the sliding glass doors displaying their badges. After briefly speaking with the nurse on duty, they headed for intensive care.

Rainbow's room was in the ICU section of the hospital. Johnson and Hernandez entered the room, recognizing only Cassandra amongst the many grim faces.

Floral arrangements were everywhere, giving the room a personality. Cassandra was seated by the bed, along with Lorraine, who'd left work early to be by her homegirl's side for support.

Vern and JP stood off in a corner staring at their homeboy's lifeless body, wondering how this tragedy would affect his blossoming musical career. They had no problem getting work from other artists, but Rainbow was something special.

Huddled up in the opposite corner were his brothers Rodney and Rufus, along with their wives Elaine and Maxine. Rodney was the eldest sibling and stood six-three. He was built like a rock of granite, soft-spoken and generous with both his time and money. A carpenter by trade, "Rod" also coached little league baseball and took all the neighborhood children on field trips to amusement parks, sporting events, rap concerts, and the library. To most people, he was considered a gentle giant. He wore a tight-fitting white t-shirt that displayed his powerful chest, blue Levi 501s, tan work boots, and a Warriors golf cap. His wife Elaine was decked out in a gray two-piece skirt suit along with stockings, gray Brazilian shoes, and matching handbag. Her blouse was white with ruffles covering the buttons, and the girl was phine. She had chiseled legs, a cream complexion, firm behind, and a mushroom-styled hairdo.

Rod and Elaine had been married for twenty years but were a couple for as long as anyone could remember.

Elaine would teach girls how to sew, fix hair, cook meals, and exhibit proper etiquette. She was employed as an executive secretary for the State of California, a job she'd held since graduating Magna Cum Laude from Berkeley. Her salary combined with the large chunks of money Rod made building houses provided them with the finer things in life. They spent most of it on other folks' kids, along with their own two children.

Rufus and Maxine were a different story. She was the major breadwinner so since she had the gold, she made the rules. "Max" worked as a supervisor for A.C. Transit bus company and was used to giving orders at work, which carried over into her personal life. She'd clown Rufus in a minute because he couldn't hold a job. His vice was weed, and he'd smoke joints the way most tobacco users smoke cigarettes. Bouncing around from job to job, Rufus would always get fired because of his mouth. He thought he knew more than his employers and would tell them what they needed to do to increase business. This, along with the fact he usually returned from lunch reeking of marijuana, always got him terminated.

Rochelle sat on the far side of the bed next to Pearlie Mae whispering "yes lord" and "amen" as her mother read bible scriptures. Rochelle was drunk.

"Detectives Johnson and Hernandez."

Cassandra was surprised.

"Miss Jones," they said in unison.

"Ms. Pearlie Mae, this is detective Johnson and Hernandez. They're the ones who solved your son Stoney's murder case," Cassandra stated proudly.

"Hello," Pearlie Mae greeted them.

The detectives nodded their heads as Cassandra introduced each person in the room. Focusing in on Rainbow, Johnson asked, "Has the doctor told you what his condition is?"

"They say it's too early to tell, but since the bullet shattered his cheekbone, he'll probably have a speech problem," Cassandra responded.

Vern and JP shook their heads in sympathy. Rainbow lay motionless with an IV unit attached to his arm replenishing his body with fluid. Tubes were placed in his nostrils, and the side of his face was covered with a gauze pad and medical tape.

Hernandez browsed through his notebook and spotted something. Excusing himself as he tapped his partner on the shoulder, they went into the hallway.

"What you got, Manny?"

"Nate, her ex, one Calvin Jones a.k.a. Shakey Jones, was scheduled to be released from Quentin last week. If so, then he becomes our number-one suspect. I wanted to ask her about him in there," he pointed at the room, "but I don't want Rainbow's folks ganging up on the girl."

"Good deal, man. We'll question her after we run a check on Shakey."

Just as they were about to re-enter the room, a doctor walked up with clipboard in hand. He had blond hair, blue eyes, a muscular physique, and youthful appearance. Johnson displayed his badge, looked at the guy's name tag, then began: "Hello Dr. Stevenson. I'm Sargeant Johnson; this is my partner Sargeant Hernandez, OPD."

"Gentlemen, what can I do for you?" the doctor said as he shook their hands.

"We'd like to know the status of Mr. Jordan."

"Oh, he'll be fine in due time."

"What about his speech?"

"Well, there will be complications with his speech pattern, no doubt. But with physical therapy, he should be back to normal in about a year."

"Speech-wise?" Johnson was leading.

"Correct! Now as far as his appearance goes, his face will not be pleasant-looking initially but after a series of skin grafts, my patient will look just fine."

"Doc ... I'm curious to know how he could get shot in an empty parking lot at a mall and nobody saw a thing," Manny stated while glancing over his notes.

"Well, sir, the trajectory of the bullet's impact was on a downward spiral, meaning that whoever shot him was on a roof. A classic sniper attempt at murder."

"Thanks doc, and if you think of anything else, give us a call." Johnson handed him a card.

"You bet," the doctor replied as he entered the room.

Nate and Manny headed for the exit, quietly discussing their strategy. Hopping in the car, they rolled back to police headquarters to do some investigating. Marching up to the second floor, they entered CID, or the Criminal Investigations Division. Johnson stormed into the Area 3 section and boomed, "Who's investigating the murder attempt at Eastmont?"

"I am," Rollins responded. "Why do you ask?"

"I need to see the report," Johnson stated.

"For what?" Rollins returned.

"Dex, I want to determine where the shot came from."

"Don't you guys have murders to solve?" Rollins' voice was laced with sarcasm.

"Yes, but we think this case ties into the other three," Johnson lied.

"Be my guest," he said, handing over the report.

Dexter Rollins, a twenty-year man, had been a sargeant for the past ten. He had taken the Lieutenant's exam several times but was never selected. No matter how high his name rose on the eligible list, he would always be passed over.

Rollins was an individual in a team environment, had a lousy attitude, and thought himself to be a genius. To him, everyone was inferior. Johnson took the report from Rollins, made two copies, then gave it back.

He and Manny went to their office, both reading as they walked. Once there, they sat down and poured over every detail with a fine-tooth comb.

"Jimmy was the tech on the case," Johnson said to his partner.

"Let's go talk to him!" Manny said.

They rode the elevator down to the basement and made a beeline to the evidence room. Once they entered, a strong aroma of weed filled their nostrils. Row after row of shelves was lined with marijuana, cocaine, methamphetamines, money, guns, televisions, and everything else taken during arrests. The smaller items were ziplock-bagged and labeled, with the larger ones just displaying tags. These items would be presented in court as evidence to help make the case, then when they were of no further use, returned to their rightful owners, donated to charity organizations, or destroyed.

Jimmy was seated at a table having lunch, which consisted of a Tupperware container filled with steamed rice and covered with a few scraps of meat and vegetables. He ate with chopsticks.

"Jimmy, we didn't know you were at lunch," Johnson said.

"It's alright," Jimmy rose and shook each man's hand. "What can I do for you guys?"

Wah Woon Chang was his given name but everyone called him Jimmy. He was Chinese, five foot eight, and stood on a thin one-hundred-and-fifty-pound frame. His rectangular glasses sat low on his nose, and a black crew-cut hairstyle covered an upside-down pyramid-shaped head.

Jimmy was well liked throughout the department, and he was the one of the best crime lab techs to ever work there. The dude was meticulous, efficient, and seemed to find evidence that most techs would overlook.

"Jimmy, we need to know where the shot came from," Manny said, handing him the paper.

"Oh yes, the shot was fired from house on Halliday Street, upstairs bedroom."

"Any evidence?" Johnson asked.

"No, just broken window on back door," Jimmy said.

"That puts us back to square one!" Manny whined.

"Yes, hit was professional," Jimmy countered.

The word "professional" sent off signals to both detectives.

"Slack!" Johnson shouted.

"Yes amigo, Shakey's homeboy," Hernandez chimed in.

"Thank you, Jimmy, sorry to interrupt your lunch." Johnson was sincere.

"Hey, no problem."

Jimmy washed his hands at the sink then sat down to resume his meal. Johnson and Hernandez strode out the swinging doors into the hallway.

"What's our next move, Nate?"

"First put a tail on Slack, find out Shakey's address, then go visit Miss Harris."

Each man had spent the weekend cold-calling all the names on the list provided by Vanessa. The more people they talked to, the more it became apparent Vanessa had lied. She'd been with Alvin until the night he died. What she was afraid of, they didn't know, but they were determined to find out.

Manny placed a call to San Quentin, asking them to fax a copy of Shakey's release papers. Looking them over, he wrote down the address in his notepad. It was Nadine's place.

Since it was getting close to their lunch hour, they drove down the block to Mexicali Rose for dinner. Johnson chose a corner booth. Hernandez slid in across from him.

"Nate? I would like nothing better than to nail Slack's ass to the wall."

"Me too, Manny, but we need something solid."

The waitress appeared, pouring them water along with

placing chips and salsa dip on the table. Johnson dipped his chips in the green sauce while Hernandez went with the hotter red version. After the waitress took their order, they resumed their conversation.

"Why you think she lied?" Manny asked Nate.

"I don't know, but I'd guess that she probably witnessed the murder and knows she could be next."

"I think it has to be something else, amigo."

"Why?" Johnson was curious.

"Because, if she was a witness to something that brutal, she would be dead too!"

Johnson pondered his partner's last statement carefully. Cops always dissected a case like this, so to them talking casually about murder was routine. Before he could respond, the waitress returned with their food. They ate in their usual silence.

Johnson left a two-dollar tip on the table, paid for both their meals, then waited in the car while Hernandez relieved himself in the restroom. Once Manny joined his partner, they went back to headquarters and requested that twenty-four-hour surveillance be placed on Robert "Slack" Henderson.

That done, they drove to the east side to pay Vanessa a surprise visit. Flashing their badges to the security guard at the gate, Johnson wheeled the car into a visitor's stall. Casually striding up to the door, Hernandez rang the bell.

"Can I help you?" Vanessa asked.

"Ms. Harris, we have a few questions we'd like to ask you. May we come in?" Johnson softly inquired.

"OK, officer."

Vanessa unlocked the security gate looking disgusted as the two nosy cops entered her home. Closing the door, she turned to face them. Manny's jaw dropped as he turned around from the fish tank. Vanessa wore a one-piece bone-colored leotard that looked as if it had been painted on. Her nipples bulged out, resembling two eyeballs, and her butt showed no panty line.

Hernandez felt his meat rise to instant attention and could not pull his gaze away from her statuesque physique. Johnson viewed his notes, willing himself not to look at the fabulous frame before him. He took a seat at the kitchen table while Manny remained standing.

Vanessa joined Johnson at the table, well aware of the trance her body held on his partner.

"Ms. Harris, I just need some information," Nate stated.

"I told you all I knew last time," she said while looking at her nails.

"Not *all* you know!" His voice emphasized the word "all."

"Yes, I did," she shot back.

"OK, let's start from the top. When was the last time you saw Jenkins?"

"Like I said before, me and Alvin broke up three weeks ago."

"Look, young lady, we've questioned everyone on the list you provided and have witnesses who will testify in court that you were with Alvin until the night he was murdered."

"Whoever told you that is a damned liar!" Her voice rose an octave.

"You were with him at a nightclub."

"No, I wasn't."

"You know who did it, don't you?"

"No!" she screamed.

"Did they threaten you?"

"Did who threaten me?"

"Look, I'll ask the questions, you give the answers, dig?"

"Man, I don't have no answers."

"Miss Harris?" His voice was soft. "We know that you know something, we just don't know why you won't tell it. We also know that more than one person committed the crime. Now my partner thinks you witnessed the entire thing. Is he correct?"

"Man, she don't know shit!" Big Ed said, barging out of the bedroom.

"Who, sir, are you?" Manny inquired.

Johnson rose to his feet while Hernandez eased his notepad inside his coat pocket and placed his hand on his revolver.

"I'm her man, and the night you refer to, she was with ME."

"What's your name, sir?" Johnson asked.

"Ed Tatum."

"Did you know Alvin Jenkins?"

"Hey man.

"That's Officer Johnson."

Big Ed and Nate faced each other while Manny stood at the ready. Vanessa sat surprised by the entire series of events.

"Look, Officer Johnson, you and your partner cain't be comin 'round here harassing my woman. She tole y'all she don't know nothing!" Big Ed was angry.

"Maybe she'd like to tell us at the station?" Johnson growled.

"Maybe she wouldn't," Big Ed snarled.

"Look, sir, we don't want a confrontation, just answers."

"Well, we ain't got none, so if y'all ain't got no search warrant OR if you ain't here to arrest nobody, then we'll have to ask you to leave."

Big Ed took Vanessa's hand and pulled her next to him in a show of solidarity. Johnson and Hernandez headed for the door, but before they walked out Johnson warned, "We'll be back!"

They marched out the door while Big Ed stood looking defiant. Vanessa wrapped her arms completely around his body while glaring menacingly at the nosy cops.

"Nate, I told you she knew something," Manny said on the way to the car.

"Yeah, Manny. I think that guy knows more."

"Let's go find out about Mister Tatum."

"I agree, partner," Johnson boomed.

They hopped in the car and sped to headquarters.

"Yeah, baby, see, da police cain't do shit unless you let 'em," Big Ed boasted.

"Ooh, don't I know it now," she chimed.

"Let's go to bed."

Big Ed led Vanessa to the bedroom. She loved the fact that he was now her man and she would not have to share him with anyone. By the time they reached the bed, her vagina was soaking wet with anticipation. She stripped down and waited patiently while her man undressed. Tonight, she would most definitely serve him right.

13
UNFINISHED BUSINESS

Shakey arose at the crack of dawn and headed for the bathroom to urinate. Returning to the room, he dropped to the floor and began doing push-ups. Satisfied with his work, he turned on his back to do sit-ups when he noticed Sheila watching his every move.

"Like what you see?" he asked.

"No, I love what I see," she answered.

"So that means you love the way I make you feel?"

"Yes! The only man who could do that to me was my husband."

"So that means mah name is at da top of yo list, huh?"

"I don't have a list," she laughed.

"Wit me you don't need one, either."

"I sure don't." She was in love.

"Where yo husband at?"

"He's dead."

Rising out of bed, Sheila grabbed a skimpy black negligee and pulled it over her head. Her long legs, wide hips, flat stomach, and round behind aroused Shakey instantly. He stood up, pulled her close, then stuck his tongue deep into her mouth. Her body responded with years of pent-up passion but she pulled away.

"Let me go to the bathroom."

"Hurry back, baby," Shakey grinned.

"I will," she said, looking over her shoulder.

As Sheila's behind switched out of the room, Shakey felt like his manhood would explode. She'd given him the best loving he had ever gotten, and it wasn't because of the newness. The inside of her body was a raging inferno, and as he banged away, she matched him stroke for stroke. He knew it would be hard for any man to satisfy this woman, but of course, he was not ordinary.

She entered the room and upon seeing his baseball bat, walked over to the bed in a trance. Shakey mounted her and within minutes had her whispering his name, along with professing her love for him. He rode her for half an hour, with her loving every minute of it. She knew he was the one and would do anything for him. Sweat poured off both of their bodies, and when he finally came, she did too. They both were asleep in less than five minutes.

Two hours later, her alarm clock went off, interrupting her beautiful dream. Shakey lay behind her in the spoon position with one hand holding both of her breasts while the other rested under her neck. Sheila slid out of bed, put on her houserobe, then went to get her children ready for school.

"Mama?"

"What, Jamal?" she asked her son.

"Who is that in your bed?"

"That's my friend, baby."

"That's not Marcus."

"He's my new friend."

"What's his name?"

"His name is Shakey."

"Shakey?" He twisted his face. "What kind of name is that?" His sister laughed.

"It's his nickname—now you finish that toast and get to school, boy."

"Oh-kayyy," he whined.

Jamal was eight and his sister Jazmine seven. Like all kids that young, they were curious, with a need to make sense out of everything. Sheila knew they didn't understand how Shakey could be in her bed today when Marcus was in it last week.

She phoned her job faking illness, then slipped into a pink jogging suit.

"Baby, I'm taking the kids to school. I'll be right back." Her voice was sensuous.

"OK, I'mo take a shower," Shakey stated.

Sheila leaned over and kissed him on the lips. Her breath was fresh from toothpaste and mouthwash. His was filthy, but she didn't care. Once the front door closed, Shakey leaped out of bed and went to the bathroom. After showering and rinsing out his mouth, he put on his sweatsuit and went outside for some fresh air. Slack was already out, and upon seeing his road dog, he let a smile crease his mug, then walked over to the other side of the court.

"Shake, boy, you somethin else," he said while taking a swig of his T-bird.

"Slack, you need ta be me fa one day, den at least you'll die in peace cause 'Lon would definitely kill yo ass, niggah!" They hugged.

"Shidd, niggah, I'ont wanna be you!"

"Why not?"

"'Cause I'm content fuckin da same woman every nite! But yo ass spread dick like ah spread peanut butter. Hell, you probly don't even know her lass name, much less middle!" They cracked up.

"Naw, ah don't. Don't need to 'cause ah know her ass," he bragged while grabbing his crotch.

"Man, you too much," Slack chided before turning serious. "Dude, what Big Ed wont wit you lass night?"

"Slackaroni, dem foos tried ta tell me ah cain't sell dope on mah goddamn co'nah."

"Dass what ah thought."

"You seen 'em?"

"Yeah, ah seen 'em, den ah left a callin card." Slack was matter-of-fact.

"Slack, what you done did?"

"Popped dat ass, what else?"

"Who? Big Ed?" Shakey hoped he would say yes.

"Naw, dat niggah didn't show his face, but ah did get Vinny, Bulldog, and Babypit."

Slack grinned while drinking some more breakfast. Shakey absorbed what he'd just heard and began formulating his strategy. He knew this meant he would have to watch his back. He had to admit he admired Slack because killing didn't bother his conscience, and someone else always got blamed for it. In this case, that someone was him.

"Dude," Shakey spoke softly, "dis what we gone do. You follow me ta Nadine's, den when ah go in and get mah clothes, you watch mah back."

"Shake, ah don't thank dass a good plan."

"Why not?"

"'Cause dass da first place dem niggahs gone look."

Shakey pondered his last statement, then concurred. "Slack, ah thank you right." He stroked his goatee.

"Shake, what you have ta do is spin some of yo dope money an buy a ride plus clothes."

"What about Nadine's car?"

"Ditch da muafucka."

"Slack, ah jus don't wont dem niggahs ta thank ah'm scared."

"Man, it ain't about bein scared, it's about stayin clean from Five-O."

Just then, Sheila pulled into the court's parking lot and got out. They watched her walk up the stairway.

"Whatup, Sheila Rae!" Slack greeted.

"Good morning, Slack," Sheila said.

Sheila gave Shakey a bear hug along with a kiss, while Slack looked on with envy. Secretly, he always dreamed of sampling Sheila's body; now he knew his dream would remain a fantasy.

"Hey baby, I'll be right back," Shakey told her.

"Do you need anything?" she questioned.

"Just yo love."

She melted in his arms as he kissed her passionately. Forcing himself away from her, Shakey walked down the stairs with Slack right behind. Slack got in his bucket and drove around the corner, easing up right behind Shakey.

"Dude, you need to get the car washed!" Slack yelled out the window.

"Why?" Shakey asked.

Slack got out and left the motor running.

"Because if Five-O finds this piece of shit, yo fingerprints gone be all on it."

"Sho you right." Shakey gave him five.

They headed to a detail shop on 14th and Center, where Slack volunteered to clean the interior. The workers found this amusing, thinking Slack was a fool. Since he used soap and water instead of Armor-All, they knew he was crazy.

Shakey paid them their easy money, put on the latex gloves Slack had given him, and drove off. He took the car to the lower bottoms, parked it, then got in with Slack, tossing the gloves. Slack polished off his liquor and flung the bottle out the window. They both knew that by night-fall, Nadine's car would be stripped naked for parts.

The "lower bottoms," also known as the "boondocks," were located in the deepest part of the west side. This was where the poorest of the poor resided. Covering the area from 7th to West Grand, down to the shipyards and train station, here one found only shacks, transient hotels, and auto wrecking yards, along with recycling centers.

"Slackaroni, you alright."

"Thanks, dawg," Slack smiled.

"Shidd, ah never would'a thought about washin off dose fanga-prints, shidd."

Slack cruised down 14th to Adeline, hooked a left, then headed home. They got out of the bucket, giving each other a bear hug.

"If you need me just hollah," Slack said.

"Know dass right," Shakey smiled.

Slack headed home for breakfast and a fresh bottle of wine. Shakey went up the opposite stairwell to Sheila's home. The door was unlocked so he entered, inhaling the sweet aroma of bacon frying.

"Damn, it smell good in here!" he yelled.

"Breakfast will be ready in a minute, babes," she smiled.

Shakey observed the menu, gave her a kiss, then washed his hands at the sink. Sheila finished cooking the bacon, eggs, O'Brien potatoes, and biscuits while he watched.

Once Sheila sat the plates on the table, Shakey spun her around and kissed her hungrily. Sheila's body was on fire. Shakey led her to the sink and in one motion bent her over, pulled down her sweats, then rammed his pole into her hot body.

They made passionate love right there with him taking her doggy style. He rammed her with so much force that her feet lifted completely off the floor. Blasting off his load, Shakey zipped up his pants and sat down to eat, not bothering to wash his hands or body. Sheila remained bent over the sink gasping for breath while liquid poured from her body, splattering onto the linoleum tile.

"Baby!" he spoke.

"Yes," she answered huskily.

"Take me to look for a car."

"OK, but what about the car you have?" She was confused.

"That ain't mine. Matter of fact, ah just took it back."

"Where do you want to go?"

"Probly San Leandro—they got a lot of used-car lots out there."

Sheila wiped up her mess with paper towels, washed her hands, then ate with her man. While she washed the dishes and mopped, Shakey sprawled out on the sofa. When her work was done, they headed to the used-car dealerships.

Shakey test-drove a few cars from several lots before deciding on a blue '83 Coupe de Ville. Since he'd led the dealers to believe the car was for Sheila, she filled out the paperwork, along with calling her insurance company to request a multi-car policy.

He wandered outside, pulled out his cell phone, and called Nadine's house, only to be greeted by her voice-mail. Furious, he hung up and joined Sheila back in the office.

The salesman folded the registration papers in half then taped it to the lower front window on the passenger side. Shakey slid into the driver's seat beaming with pride. Handing Sheila five hundred dollars, he gave her instructions.

"Here, take this money and go buy me a few pair of jeans, a couple of sweatsuits, and some underwear."

"You need socks and cologne?" she asked.

"Yeah, get me some of that, too. If you run out of money, just get what you can."

"What size do you wear in pants?"

"Thirty-four, thirty-six."

"OK, baby." She leaned over and kissed him.

Hopping into her Hyundai, Sheila rolled to Bayfair Mall. She felt proud of the fact that she would dress her man. The only male she had shopped for in years was her son Jamal. Now instead of buying boys' clothes, she would be in the men's section.

Shakey cruised down East 14th with the windows down and rap music blaring from the sound system. Making a right turn at High Street then a left at Agua Vista, he parked in front of Rainbow's house.

Nadine had given him the address, which caused him to wonder why she hadn't paged or answered her phone. Maybe Slack was right, he thought. He got out of the car and headed up to the door, knowing Rainbow wouldn't be answering. Slack made sure of that.

Cassandra heard the doorbell ring and peeped out from behind the curtain. Seeing Shakey standing there, her heart sunk. Lorraine and Mona had told everyone at work what happened, so her boss gave her a few days off to get her business in order.

"What do you want, Calvin?" She always called him by his given name.

"Ah wanna see mah kids."

"They ain't here."

"Look Sandy, I ain't foe no games."

"Calvin, they're not here!" she shouted.

"Gurl, open da doe."

"I ain't opening shit."

"You don't open it, I'll break it down!" he screamed.

"If you do some shit like that, I'll call the police. The kids are staying with mama in San Diego, so they ain't here. Now just leave!"

"Awight, I'mo leave, but I'll damn sho be back."

Shakey pounded the heel of his fist on the door before heading back to his new ride. Peeling rubber, he screeched away from the curb. Paying too much attention to his new car along with being angry at Cassandra, Shakey failed to notice that he was not alone.

Flea shifted into drive and tailed from half a block behind. Donnie rode shotgun, with Billy Ray occupying the back seat. Their instructions from Big Ed were to find out Shakey's crib location.

Shakey obliged by driving directly to Chestnut Court. Since Sheila wasn't home, he went to Slack's house. Yolanda sat at the kitchen table picking red beans. The scent of neckbones boiling permeated the air.

"Damn, seems like ah came right on time," Shakey said.

"Whatup Shake? Seems like Sheila Rae gone be doin yo cookin!" Yolanda gave him a hug.

"Gurll, you need an agent!"

"Fa what?" she smiled.

"Yo comedy career."

"Aw, fuck you, niggah."

"If you did, Slack would be homeless."

They hugged again, squeezing each other tight. Shakey

loved the repartee he and Yolanda shared—they were like siblings.

"Slack, baby, God's gift to women is here," she yelled.

"Thank you," Shakey deadpanned.

Yolanda could only laugh at his last statement. She resumed her spot at the table as Slack entered the living room.

"Whatup dawg?" Slack said while wiping his eyes.

"Check out mah ride, boy."

"What you get?" Slack asked as they headed outside.

"A Caddy, what else?" Shakey bragged.

Shakey and Slack went downstairs to his car and looked it over when all of a sudden Slack got quiet.

"Slackaroni, ah know you wont one uh dese, but damn, don't go on mute."

"Shake, don't look now, but ain't dat da same Fleet-wood Big Ed's boys be rollin in?"

Slack pointed at the tires while talking, giving off the impression to anyone looking that his interest was on the car. Shakey caught on, pointing at the tires then the interior.

They got in the car with Shakey peeping out Flea, Billy Ray, and Donnie.

"Yeah, das dem muthafuckas," he said to Slack. "Dey must'a followed mah ass from Sandra's."

"Dude, here's what we gonna do." Slack was serious. "We gone get out the car, act like we goin in the house, but take the walkway ta Spodie's, so ah can get mah shit. Then, when we get back, you go upstairs ta mah place and I'll go blow dey ass ta hell."

"Good deal, Slack."

They half-walked, half-ran to Spodie's garage. Slack strapped himself to the max, along with giving Shakey a Glock "just in case" he needed it. Stopping at Mohammed's, Slack purchased two bottles of wine and a Sprite as Shakey stood at the door.

Shakey glared menacingly at Mohammed, who refused to look his way. Slack paid the man then strutted out. Pouring out the liquid from one bottle of T-bird, he refilled it with soda, handing it to his friend.

"Das cause ah know you don't drank," Slack said, smiling.

"Thanks dawg, know ah cain't be gettin drunk roun heah," Shakey responded.

"Dude, you go back the way we came."

"What about you?"

"Ah'mo take West Grand an sneak up on dose basthads."

"What about 'Lon?"

"Tell her ah'm on a mission—she'll know." Slack was positive.

"Be safe, bro," Shakey hugged him.

Each man walked off in opposite directions.

14
A FRIEND IN NEED

Rainbow rolled over writhing in excruciating pain. He didn't remember being shot but knew that must have been what happened, considering his condition. His breath was hot, body sticky, and room unfamiliar, but what he wanted right now were pain pills.

His head felt as though it would explode at any moment. Feeling his hand around for the remote control switch, he pushed the call button for the nurse.

Wiping the matter from his eyes, he focused. The frame silhouetted before him displayed unfamiliar legs, but they looked delicious. Peering upwards, he was surprised to see Lorraine.

"Heyyy gurlll," he slurred.

"How are you?" Lorraine asked.

"I'm f-f-fine," he stuttered. "Where Cah-Cah-Cassandra at?" he blurted.

"I don't know. She took the week off from work because of your accident. I thought she would be here—that's why I came!"

"Oh, you d-d-didn't come fo m-m-me?"

"Baby, stop trying to talk, OK? Just lay there."

Lorraine rose out of her seat to comfort Rainbow, then decided to give him a hug. Kissing his forehead, she whispered, "I'm here for you, dude."

"Th-th-thank you, gurllll."

Lorraine was decked out in a brown two-piece skirt suit accented by a dark brown turtleneck sweater, matching shoes, and leather purse. The nurse entered the room, immediately assuming that Lorraine was Rainbow's woman.

"Oh, we have a visitor. My name is Margie."

"I'm Lorraine."

"Honey, I need your help," she stated.

"With what?" Lorraine asked.

"First, I need to change the bandages on your husband's face. Then I need to give him a sponge bath."

"OK, but he's not my husband, we're just friends."

Margie gave Rainbow his pain medication and checked his blood pressure, pulse, and temperature. As she started the process of changing his bandages, she took extreme care to stress the importance of this daily procedure.

The hole in Rainbow's face resembled a piece of raw meat. Lorraine felt sick to the stomach seeing it. She was impressed by the way the nurse cleaned and disinfected the wound with ointment as if it were just another work routine.

"Time to go to the bathroom, Mister Jordan. Sweetie,

you help me give him his sponge bath," the nurse said to Lorraine.

They both lifted Rainbow up by the armpits and escorted him to the shower. Margie rolled the pole holding the bag of liquid that continuously pumped fluid into his body. They went inside the restroom, where she filled a small plastic tub with mild soap and lukewarm water, then pulled down his gown to his waist and washed his upper body and legs.

"I'll leave you to wash his private parts," she said, winking to Lorraine as she sauntered out the door.

Pangs of guilt overwhelmed Lorraine as she thought about carrying out the nurse's instructions. Suddenly an idea popped into her head.

"Rainbow, I need to make a phone call!"

"Oh k-k-kay," he stammered.

She walked out, leaving the door open with him in full view. She knew if Cassandra caught her bathing Rainbow, their friendship would be over, not to mention her reputation at work.

"Hello." Cassandra's voice was dry.

"Girl, what's wrong?" Lorraine asked.

"Nothing."

"Sandy, what's wrong?"

"That fool showed up."

"Shakey?" Lorraine whispered.

"Yes—came here asking about the kids."

"What you say?"

"I told his black ass that they weren't here."

"What he say?"

"Fool say he gone be back. Lo, where you at?"

"I'm at the hospital."

"With Rainbow?

"Yes! What time you comin?"

"What he doin?" Cassandra asked.

"He's asleep—what time you comin?"

"Gurll, Shakey done made me so mad I ain't coming to the hospital today."

"You're not?" Lorraine was surprised.

"Naw, I'mo go play bingo tonight. I need to get my mind together."

"Do you need me to do anything?"

"Yes, girl," Cassandra said.

"What?"

"Give my man a kiss for me and tell him I have a headache."

"Gurlll, you be careful," Lorraine warned.

"OK."

"Bye."

"Bye, bye."

Lorraine returned to the restroom, gave Rainbow a kiss on the cheek, then closed the door. She dipped the sponge, wrung it out, then lifted up his gown. She'd seen naked men before, but she felt very awkward with him. She knew what she was doing was wrong, but she also knew Cassandra was a user and not right for this man.

Cassandra was the type of woman who could have a good man all to herself but would be too stupid to realize it. Over the years Lorraine had witnessed her friend find something wrong with every man she'd met, failing to realize that nobody's perfect.

Rainbow looked directly into Lorraine's eyes as she washed his groin area and behind. She caught his gaze and could not force herself to break the spell. The brief time she'd spent with him in Reno remained fresh in her mind. He was a good man. She could only presume that he had not seen the real Sandy because if he had, he would have dropped her like a hot potato. Leading him to the facebowl, she filled a plastic cup with mouthwash. Tilting his head backward, she poured some in his mouth.

"Rinse," she demanded.

Rainbow's mouth was on fire. He leaned forward, letting the wash dribble off his lips.

"Baby, you have to let it work."

"It's work . . . ing," he said.

"Not that quick—here take some more."

She poured another dose, holding his chin up where he would either have to gurgle or swallow. He held it in as long as he could before leaning over, watching it splatter in the bowl.

"Come on, let me take you back to your bed," she told him.

"Oh k-k-kay."

Lorraine helped Rainbow to bed, then sat in a chair next to him.

"Thank you," Rainbow whispered.

"You're welcome" she answered.

"What time is Cah-Cah—"

"She has a headache."

"Oh, she ain't c-c-coming?"

"No, she's not."

Lorraine flicked on the television screen then tucked Rainbow in. Taking a magazine from her purse she began to read silently. Five minutes later Rainbow was sleeping like a baby.

The doctor entered the room, spoke to Lorraine, then walked out. Before the door closed, in came Pearlie Mae and Rochelle.

"Hi," said Lorraine.

"Hi baby," Pearlie Mae returned.

Lorraine rose to embrace Pearlie, whose body language suggested that she was about to give a hug. Rochelle stood with hands on hips, looking evil.

"You're Cassandra's friend, right?" Rochelle asked.

"Yes, I am."

"Where's she at?"

"Oh, she has a headache, so she won't be coming today."

"You know, that might be yo friend an all, but I'mo tell it like it is—that girl is a snake."

"Oh really?"

"Hell yeah, and ah don't give a damn if you go back and tell her cause all ah need is reason ta get in her ass anyway."

"Rochelle!" Pearlie Mae hollered.

"Mama, I'm just telling it like it is," Rochelle pleaded.

"Guhl, don't nobody wanna be hearin dat ghetto mess ta-day."

"OK, moms." Rochelle wandered into the restroom.

"Baby, mah name is Pearlie Mae and don't you be payin Rochelle no mind, OK?"

"Yes ma'am. I'm Lorraine."

Rochelle returned from the restroom with a plastic cup, lifted a bottle of wine from her purse, then filled the cup. Taking a swig, she resumed her assault on Cassandra.

"Hey sis, I'm sorry if I offended you, but somebody needs to call a spade a spade. My name is Rochelle."

"I'm Lorraine." They touched hands.

"Now correct me if I'm wrong, but don't this look funny?"

"Don't what look funny?"

"That you here and she not."

"I guess it does, but she didn't know I was coming."

"And you didn't know she wasn't."

With that line they both burst out laughing. Secretly Lorraine knew Rochelle had a point. She liked her already. They filled the next twenty minutes with small talk. A stranger would have thought these two ladies had been friends for years, never knowing they had just met two days ago.

Pearlie Mae lifted her book from her purse and began reading scriptures, out loud as usual.

"The Lord is my shepherd, I shall not want.

The door swung open, with all eyes looking to see who the visitor would be. Rodney entered the room grinning.

CLOSING IN

The detectives rolled to the station still angry at Big Ed. They were met at the door by Moroski and Colvin.

"Hey guys, what's cooking?" Manny asked.

"We have another murder," Moroski responded.

"Good lord," Manny whistled. "Where?"

"On the east side! Victim was asphyxiated; name is Nadine McCoy. Prime suspect is one Calvin Jones a.k.a. Shakey; suspect was the victim's boyfriend. Get this, he was just released from the pen six days ago. More than likely he found out she wasn't faithful," Colvin speculated with a smirk.

"Where's Shakey now?" Johnson asked.

"Don't know," Moroski said to Manny, ignoring Johnson.

John Moroski and Peter Colvin were the number-two detective team behind Johnson and Hernandez. Best buddies, they were of the same mindset. They were both racist and considered Manny the lesser of two evils.

Moroski stood six foot six, weighed three hundred pounds, and had blond hair and blue eyes. He was nicknamed "Pumpkin" throughout the department because many of the suits he wore were too tight. Colvin was six four with red hair, brown eyes, freckles on his face, and a powerful two-hundred-and-sixty-pound frame. His nickname was "Skeeter Red." Both men were just as large as Johnson and hated his guts equally. They lived on the same block in predominantly white Walnut Creek and referred to Oaktown as "the jungle."

Johnson knew that since he was the senior detective, Moroski should be addressing him instead of Manny, but he also knew Moroski and Colvin didn't give a shit about protocol. They both were respected throughout the department and damn good at their job.

"You guys don't mind if we tag along, do you?" Nate's question was more of a statement.

"Suit yourself," Colvin said. "Matter of fact, if you want the case, it's yours."

"We'll take it," Johnson deadpanned.

Colvin walked over to the case board and erased his and Moroski's names, replacing them with "Johnson and Hernandez." Nate and Manny left the office without a thank you or goodbye, which their two co-workers knew wouldn't be for real anyway. Bad blood filled the air every time these four detectives crossed paths. One day it would boil over. They all knew it but none seemed to care.

Rolling back to the east side, Johnson and Hernandez

pulled up in front of Nadine's apartment, only to be met by the usual horde of reporters. Exiting the car, Johnson held up the palm of his right hand.

"Ladies and gentlemen, we will give you a full report once we complete our investigation."

He and Manny walked past the media into Nadine's house. The evidence techs were busy dusting for finger-prints, snapping photos, and examining her body. They looked for skin under fingernails, semen on the skin, hair strands—anything that could be DNA-tested.

"Anything to work with?" Johnson asked no one in particular.

"Just a little, Sarge," the female officer answered.

"What have you got, Stacy?"

"There was no sign of forced entry. Her closet is stocked with men's clothing that was purchased recently, and we also found prison release papers." She closed her note-book.

"The name would be Calvin Jones?" Manny asked.

"Yes, sir," Stacy confirmed.

"Put out an APB on Jones," Johnson ordered as he walked outside to address the media.

An all-points bulletin was announced throughout the city for Shakey. As the message blared over police blot-ters, Foster and McDavid spotted what they considered a possible suspect. McDavid shifted the car into drive and mashed the accelerator.

The vehicle lurched forward with tires squealing. Fos-ter was out of the car before it stopped with his gun drawn.

"Freeze! OPD!" he screamed. "Put your hands in the

air and don't move a muscle!" he hollered.

"Man, I ain't did nothing!" Shakey shouted while raising his arms.

"Calvin Jones?" McDavid questioned as he eased up
the stairwell.

"Yeah, that's my name."

"You're under arrest!"

Chestnut Court's residents, hearing the commotion,
flooded the grounds. Jamal and Jazmine ran to Auntie
Yolanda's house to tell her the news.

"Arrest for what?" Shakey screamed.

"The murder of Nadine McCoy."

"Man, ah ain't killed nobody."

"Spread 'em!" McDavid hollered as Foster patted Shakey
down.

"Man, what yaw doin? Shakey ain't did shit!" Yolanda
yelled as she came down the stairs.

"Ma'am, please stay back," Foster ordered.

"I ain't stayin shit! Every time y'all cain't solve a damn
case, den here you come 'round heah!" she shouted.

"Ma'am, if you don't back up, I'll have to arrest you."

"It's cool, 'Lon, they ain't got shit on me," Shakey told
her.

They shoved him into the unmarked car and sped back
to headquarters, informing central dispatch of their capture. Johnson and Hernandez heard the news on their blot-
ter and zoomed to the station.

Shakey sat handcuffed to his chair as the detectives
entered the room. He was steaming. He saw absolutely
no logic to being cuffed in the interrogation room. What

he didn't know was that after Roscoe Porter's escape a memo was sent instructing all officers to handcuff suspects to the chair. This singular action would prevent further occurrences.

"Jones, we'd like to ask you a few questions," Johnson announced.

"Can you take the cuffs off first?"

"Why did you kill her?" Johnson said while uncuffing Shakey.

"Kill who?" Shakey answered while rubbing his wrists.

"You know who."

"Man, I'ont know what you talkin 'bout."

"Nadine McCoy, that's who."

"I didn't kill Nadine. Hell, I ain't even knowed she was dead til now."

"Tell me what you know about Reggie Jordan." Johnson threw a curve.

"Who?" Shakey swung and missed.

"You may know him as Rainbow."

"Rainbow?"

"Yes, the same Rainbow who's engaged to your ex-wife."

"Don't know 'im."

"What do you know, Jones?"

"I know I ain't answering no more questions until I see my lawyer!" Shakey screamed.

"Oh, you have a lawyer?" Johnson arched his brow.

"Hell yeah, and his name is Public Defender!" Shakey smiled at his own wit.

"Look punk! . . ." Johnson hollered.

"Ah got you punk awight!"

Johnson stood over Shakey while he sat passively in his chair staring at his clasped hands. Shakey knew that any flinch or movement would justify the beating they wanted to give him—at least that's what he believed.

"Listen Jones, here's the way we see it," Johnson said, sitting down at the table again and speaking softly. "First, you get out of the pen then want revenge on Rainbow, not only for taking your woman, but also because you blame him for your brother's death. So you have him killed." He lied about the killing part to see Shakey's reaction.

"Oh really?" Shakey was unfazed.

"Yes really. Next, you find out that your new main squeeze, Miss McCoy, has been giving up booty to someone else, so your ego is bruised."

"Man, that shit would make a great movie—you in the wrong profession, bro!" Shakey was smiling.

"I ain't yo bro," Johnson whispered through clenched teeth.

"Nate, let's call the public defender's office," Manny said to his partner, fearing he would lose it.

Johnson rose out of his chair, cuffed Shakey back to his, then left the room. As the door slammed Shakey was already demanding his one phone call.

Hernandez wrote in their entry and exit on the log sheet, placing it back in the slot. Nate was at the reception desk in the lobby picking up the telephone when Yolanda spotted him.

"There dey go," she told Sheila while rising to make her presence known.

"Excuse me!" she hollered to Johnson.

"Damn, if it ain't the bride of Frankenstein," Hernandez whispered.

"What can we do for you?" Johnson asked, opening the door.

"You can tell us where Shakey at."

Yolanda's hands rested on her hips and her attitude needed adjusting. Sheila stood by her with a look of disdain on her face.

"Mrs. Henderson, Mister Jones is being interrogated," Johnson said.

"Fa what?" Yolanda questioned.

"Suspicion of murder," he answered.

"Officer, excuse me, but may I ask when this murder was supposed to occur?" Sheila questioned.

"Sunday night!" Manny stated the fact.

"Well, you'll have to release him then."

"Oh, we will?" Johnson placed the receiver back on the telephone base. "And why would we do that?"

"Because Sunday night Mr. Jones was with me!"

"You're prepared to testify under oath that what you say is true?"

"Yes."

"Come with me."

Johnson led Sheila to an unoccupied interview room as Yolanda took a seat in the hallway. The next hour was spent with Sheila giving Shakey an alibi.

"So you say he got to your place about nine?" Johnson asked.

"Yes," Sheila answered.

"What if I told you that the coroner places the time of death between eight and nine P.M.?"

"Then I would say that proves he's innocent."

"Why would you say that?"

"'Cause you can't be in two places at the same time, and he was with ME!"

"Excuse us for a minute," Nate said.

He and Manny walked out leaving the door open, but whispering.

They came back and Johnson told Sheila, "OK, you're free to go. If we need any more information, we'll contact you."

"Thank you, officer," Sheila said as she walked out.

Yolanda saw Sheila coming her way then stood waiting.

"Girl, what they say?"

"They said they would call me," Sheila told her.

"When dey gone let Shake go?"

"I don't know, 'Lon."

"Sheila Rae, let's get the hell outta here. This place gives me the creeps."

They left the station and headed home.

16
DIE AS YOU LIVE

Slack lurked in the shadows of the court, peeping out the Caddy parked on Linden Street. He was sure there were three people inside, but now he saw only two. Further down the block, he noticed an unmarked police car with two cops in it. They sat low in the seats and appeared to be watching his place.

"Damn, da bastahd's followin me," he said to himself.

Contemplating his next move didn't take long because the cops decided for him by moving first. They mashed into the court, hemming up Shakey, who had just returned. The parking lot and grounds were flooded by tenants anxious to see who Five-O was rolling on today. The commotion that ensued created just the diversion Slack needed.

Springing into action with the quickness, he screwed the silencer on his Glock and headed towards his prey.

Noticing someone whom he assumed to be the third man coming from the opposite direction, Slack slowed his pace.

Flea and Billy Ray saw Donnie coming, but they had their attention on Shakey and the cops. Donnie opened the door then sprawled on the seat, courtesy of Slack's foot on his behind.

Flea and Billy Ray turned around but it was too late. Slack shot each man before they could move. Both men slumped sideways in their seat ... dead. Slack pushed the gun up to Donnie's temple and fired.

Blood shot out of his brain, ruining the carpeted floor. Closing the door, Slack headed towards Grand Avenue. The entire killing spree took less than ten seconds but was clean as a whistle.

"Mission accomplished," Slack said to himself.

He got to the corner of West Grand and thought it must be his lucky day because rolling in his direction was Sheila. Flagging her down, he got in, throwing the bags containing Shakey's new clothing on the back seat.

"Sheila Rae! Take me to Spodie's garage!" he barked.

"What's going on?" she asked with alarm.

"The police got Shakey, but they thank it's me, so I'm gone hide," he lied.

"They got Shakey?"

"Girl, just drive!" he demanded.

"OH KAYYY!" she yelled.

Sheila drove to Spodie's house with Slack giving her his fairy tale of why he was running. He damned sure wasn't going to tell her what he'd just done—he never told.

210

"I'm going to get to the bottom of this shit," she growled as he got out.

"Yeah, baby—all they need to know is Shakey been wif you."

"He HAS been with me!"

"Sheila Rae, calm down, gurlll!"

"OK, Slack," she smiled.

He closed the door as she sped back to the court, determined to find out why Five-O was clowning her man. Slack casually strode to the garage. Unlocking the door, he went in.

Sheila arrived at the complex as the rollers were driving off. Shakey twisted his head around in the seat then blew her a kiss. Yolanda stood in the court's parking lot with her hands on her hips.

"Gurll, what happened?" Sheila asked.

"Dey arrested Shakey."

"For what?"

"Say he killed dat bitch."

"The one who picked him up from prison?"

"Yeah, da bitch dead."

"Gurll, we need to go to the police station," Sheila said bluntly.

"That's why I was waitin on you. My kids can watch yours til Slack gets home. I wonder where he at, anyway?" Yolanda spoke to herself.

"Gurl, let's go," Sheila stated.

They got in the car and angrily drove to OPD headquarters. Sheila told Yolanda about her encounter with Slack, along with the lies he'd told her. Yolanda nodded, smiling. She knew Slack was up to something and would not even tell her the truth, much less Sheila Rae.

Meanwhile, back at the garage, Slack returned his unused weapons to their hiding spot. He stuffed the loaded Glock in his pants and thought about where he would dump it. Flicking off the lights, he opened the door to leave.

He took one step outside, only to be greeted by a thundering right hand. The force of the blow was so violent that it broke his nose, causing both eyes to swell immediately.

"Man, what you doin?" Slack screamed.

His question was answered by a foot to the head. He reached for the gun in his waistband but was too slow. Blows rained on his head so viciously that he used both hands to cover up for protection.

He felt his body being lifted off the floor then flung like a rag doll, slamming against the wall. Another foot caught him in the rib cage, cracking three. Slack attempted to grab his gun again but felt his arm twisted behind his back so forcefully that it snapped.

Massive fingers clutched his throat as he struggled to breathe. He tried to pry the gloved hands away, but his attempt proved futile. White foam dripped from the corners of his mouth as his body went limp.

Slack's life ended the same way he lived—violently and without warning. The door closed and the padlock snapped in place.

The Oaktown Devil would not kill again.

Rodney hopped the fence, trudging through the weeded

lot back to his truck. He had camped out at his friend Bootsy's, right across the street from Rainbow's crib.

With a bird's-eye view from the living room, he had seen Shakey clown Cassandra and prepared to follow that fool. Before he got to his car, he noticed that Flea, Billy Ray, and Donnie had the same idea, so he trailed them. Parking one block away, facing their car, he watched and waited.

When Slack flagged down Sheila Rae, Rod trailed them to Spodie's, parking around the corner. Taking a shortcut through an empty field, he waited right outside the garage door.

Rodney's logic was simple. Deadly as this fool was, if he wasn't responsible for Rainbow's shooting, the streets would be better off without him anyway. He had to die.

Tossing his leather gloves into a garbage can, Rodney glided through the sliding doors at Highland and headed for Rainbow's room. He entered the room smiling, happy to see Pearlie Mae, Rochelle, and Lorraine.

17
JUSTICE

Johnson arrived for duty thirty minutes early. He checked voicemail messages on the telephone then retrieved his written memos. There was a note from Evans in the pile marked "urgent." Crossing the hall from homicide, he entered CID. Evans spotted him coming through the door and got up to greet him.

"Hey Sarge, what's shaking?" Evans asked while shaking his hand.

"Got a memo from you, Johnny."

"Yes, it's about the Jenkins case."

"Lay it on me," Johnson said.

"Three guys were found dead in a car on the west side last night."

"Who were they?"

"Street thugs employed by the east-side empire. The victims were ambushed in their Caddy, but that's not the point."

"The point being...?"

"Sarge, we found a chainsaw in the trunk of the car with blood on it."

"DNA?" Johnson said bluntly.

"Correct! It was a perfect match to Alvin Jenkins, so what we have here is the same power tool used to chop off Jenkins' hands."

"What are the victims' names?"

"Two brothers, Billy and Donnie Barnes, along with a small-time hood named Clyde Featherstone, street tag is Flea."

"You say they worked for the east-side empire?" Johnson probed.

"Yes, sir, their boss is a dude named Edward Tatum, known throughout the hood as Bid Ed. The car is registered to Tatum."

"So they killed Jenkins."

"It looks that way, Sarge."

"Thanks, Johnny."

"You bet."

Johnson returned to homicide, where he waited on his partner. Manny entered the office with the usual stoic look on his face. When his eyes caught Johnson's, he smiled. The look on Nate's face told Manny that his partner had good news.

"OK, what's with the smirk?" Manny asked.

"What smirk is that?" Johnson displayed all thirty-two.

"That stupid look on your face."

"Good news, Manny," Johnson said.

"Lay it on me."

"What we got, Manny, is the chainsaw used to chop off Alvin Jenkins' hands."

"How did we get that?" Manny asked.

"Pure luck, man."

"Man, get to the damn point."

During the entire conversation Johnson held a knowing grin on his face. Manny knew he was having fun with this one—he would drag it out until Hernandez was tired of playing.

"OK, Nate, game's over. Now spit it out, amigo."

"Manny . . . three hoods from the east-side empire were ambushed on the west side last night. They were on their own stakeout at Slack's place, but eventually got steaked. Get this: in the trunk of the vehicle they were riding in was a chainsaw."

"And?" Manny was getting irritated.

"And, the chainsaw had dried blood on it, so the techs ran a DNA test which revealed that Jenkins' hands were chopped off by that saw."

"Wait a minute, partner. Now if the three people in the car are all dead, then that puts us right back to square one." Manny thought he had a point.

"Not exactly—the car was registered to one Edward Tatum," Johnson said proudly.

"We got that sonofabitch!" Manny shouted.

"Well, we don't really have anything except the car is owned by him."

"Let's pick his ass up anyway," Manny growled.

They took the ten-minute ride to Vanessa's condo and parked in a visitor stall. Vanessa was about to feed her fish when she saw them get out of the car.

"Baby, those two police are outside again," she said to Big Ed.

Big Ed stood in the doorway staring angrily at the two cops approaching.

"Edward Tatum?" Johnson asked while displaying his badge.

"Man, you know that's my name."

"Do you own a black Cadillac Fleetwood?"

"Yes, why?"

"Three people were killed inside your car last night," Johnson stated.

"Oh really?" Big Ed showed surprise.

"Yes, I believe they were associates of yours. Clyde Featherstone, Billy Barnes and his brother Donnie Barnes."

"They're all dead?"

"Yes, they are!"

"Who did it?" Big Ed questioned.

"We don't know, but what we would like to know is how did these gentlemen wind up in your car?"

"I let 'em use it."

"When?"

"A couple of days ago."

"Could you be more specific?"

"Friday, yeah, it was Friday," Big Ed told him.

Johnson had him dead to rights. Since the murder of Alvin Jenkins was committed on a Wednesday, Tatum could be brought in for at least seventy-two hours while they put together a case. Manny's cell phone rang so he answered the call. Speaking in hushed tones, he hung up then joined Nate, Big Ed, and Vanessa back at the door. Three patrol cars eased into the complex as Manny spoke.

"Mr. Edward Tatum and you, Miss Vanessa Harris, are under arrest!"

"Arrest?" Big Ed shouted, "For what?"

"The murder of Alvin Jenkins."

Vanessa started crying as the uniformed officers handcuffed her and Big Ed. They led her to the car then drove to headquarters.

"Why did you arrest the girl?" Johnson asked his partner.

"The techs found strands of hair in the trunk belonging to a woman, and the colors match hers."

"So she did witness the murder."

"Yes, Nate, it appears she did."

"Let's go get the truth out of her."

They rode to the station discussing their game plan. Somehow, they had to convince Vanessa to tell them what she knew about Alvin's murder. Vanessa sat in the interrogation room crying her eyes out. She felt violated by the strip search and vulnerable being caged like an animal.

Although she now loved Big Ed more than any man she'd ever known, if push came to shove, he would certainly be going to prison alone. The door opened with Johnson and Hernandez closing it behind them.

"Are you ready to tell us what you know?" Manny took the lead.

"I don't know anything," she answered.

"Look, young lady, we have strands of hair belonging

to YOU that were found in the trunk of that car." He got to the point: "We also have the chainsaw covered with Alvin's blood which was used to chop off his hands. Your alibi doesn't add up because we have witnesses who will testify in court that you were with Jenkins on the night he died."

Vanessa broke down.

"OK!" she screamed, "I'll tell you what you want to know."

"Good," Manny whispered, "Now start from the beginning."

"We went to the club that night for dancing. When we left, Billy Ray and Donnie beat us up outside and threw us in the trunk. They took us to the Point, where they killed Alvin." She broke down again while Johnson let his tape recorder run. She wiped her eyes and nose and continued, "Alvin had promised Ed a sixteen-thousand-dollar return for his two-thousand-dollar investment in the pyramid scheme, but he didn't pay it off. Once he got fresh, they killed him!"

"Who pulled the trigger?" Johnson asked.

"Billy Ray," she responded.

"Who cut off his hands?" Hernandez butted in.

"Billy and Donnie."

"What did they do with the hands?" Johnson took his turn.

"They threw them on the freeway."

"Go on," Hernandez said on cue.

"Next, they took me to my place where I gave them all the money we had.

"How much?" Johnson interrupted.

"Four thousand dollars."

"Then what?" Hernandez demanded.

"Then ... then ... then."

"Then what?" Johnson's tone was soothing.

"Then Big Ed made me have sex with him!" she blurted.

"Was it forced or consensual?" Hernandez questioned.

"I had no choice—I wanted to live."

"So he raped you?" Johnson asked softly.

"Yes," she lied, "then he told me if I ever mentioned a word of the murder to anyone, he'd kill me. He also said that I was now his woman."

Johnson and Hernandez exited the room, heading for the district attorney's office to press charges. They charged Big Ed with being an accomplice to murder, rape, and kidnapping.

They still had nothing on Shakey except the fact that at the time of Nadine's death he was on his way to Sheila's. Regardless, they would keep him in custody for the maximum seventy-two hours while they searched for clues. The murders of Flea and the gruesome twosome had been assigned to Moroski and Colvin, meaning that Nate and Manny only had to find Nadine's killer in order to close their books. They felt relieved, which was an understatement.

"How 'bout a bite to eat, amigo?" Manny asked after they left the DA's office.

"I was just about to suggest the same thing, dude," Nate answered.

The detectives strutted out of headquarters like two

peas in a pod. The two days off would definitely be welcomed. Of course, they would have Shakey tailed upon release. Laughing, they headed for Mexicali Rose, where they would eat in silence.

18
BONAFIDE SNAKE

Cassandra arrived home close to midnight, pockets empty. The money she'd taken from Rainbow's trousers at the hospital was lost at the bingo hall. It had been more than enough to last until her next payday, so now she was stuck between a rock and a hard place.

Iceberg greeted her at the garage door leading to the house, but instead of replenishing his water dish and food tray, she stormed inside. Searching the entire home for money, she still came up empty. She sat with her head on her knees feeling sorry for herself when an idea struck. Getting back into her ride, she went to the hospital.

Pulling up at Highland, she waited until the coast was clear before heading to Rainbow's room. He was asleep, so she tiptoed to the closet and retrieved his wallet. Stuffing it in her purse, she eased out the door.

Rainbow witnessed the whole scene through the slits

of his eyes. If someone had told him that his woman was a money-hungry thief, he never would have believed it. Since he saw it for himself, he knew she was not the one for him. He was hurt.

Picking up the telephone, he called all his creditors, canceling every account. He also called the bank, suspending action on his checking and savings accounts. Last, he called Rodney, asking his brother to make sure that Cassandra was out of his house before nightfall.

That done, he drifted off into a peaceful sleep. When he woke up, Lorraine was sitting next to his bed reading the morning paper. He smiled. She attempted to tell him the news reports of Shakey, Big Ed, Vanessa, and the eastside empire, but he cut her off with a hand movement.

"I luv ... luv ... luv, I love you!" he shouted.

"I love you too, Rainbow!"

She rose out of her chair and hugged him.

"Now go to w-w-w.

"I'm going," she laughed as she went to work.

Rainbow and Lorraine were married nine months later.

BABY'S MEMORY

Yolanda paced the floor all night waiting for her man to return home. It was unlike Slack to be away that long, so she was beginning to worry. She went to bed at four in the morning but couldn't sleep. Tossing and turning for the next few hours, she arose at seven with her mind made up. She would do something she'd never done: check on Slack's whereabouts.

Reaching into his nightstand drawer, she located the spare key to Spodie's garage. Getting into Slack's bucket, she drove the three-minute ride to Spodie's.

Garbage men were busy doing their job, along with the early birds speeding to work. Yolanda drove slowly, hoping for the best but thinking the worst. She pulled into the driveway, where she was met by Spodie's mom.

"Mama McKnight, how you doin?"

"Yolanda, guhl, where you been? Ah ain't seed you in

God knows how long." Mama McKnight spoke in ebonics.

"I've been fine, mama—I just came to see if Slack was around here."

"Baby, ah ain't seen Slack since dat day him an Shakey come to look at da cah."

"Well, I have the spare key so I wanted to see if he was in the garage. Ain't like him not to come home."

"OK baby, ah'll go wif you."

Yolanda and Mama McKnight went back to the garage, and Yolanda struggled with the padlock. Once she got it to work, she opened the door and flicked on the lights. The sight her eyes rested on would remain with her until the day she died. There sprawled out on the floor was Slack, badly beaten and certainly dead. Yolanda vomited on the spot, while Mama McKnight ran to the house to call the police.

Instantly, Yolanda's world was turned upside down. Now she no longer cared about all the money they'd saved, nor the money and drugs still under the hood of Spodie's Seville. Her man was dead.

Moroski and Colvin arrived on the scene, followed shortly thereafter by paramedics, evidence techs, and employees from the coroner's office. The news media arrived looking for a story line but found Yolanda to be of no help. She was like a zombie.

Mama McKnight called Sheila, who came to take her friend home. Sheila felt pangs of guilt because she was the one who'd dropped Slack off, meaning she was the last person who had seen him alive, besides the murderer.

"Sheila Rae, it ain't yo fault," Yolanda reassured her.

"But gurl, I could've done something," Sheila pleaded.

Sheila drove back to the court feeling sadder than Yolanda, who proved to be stronger than even Sheila Rae thought. Before the day was over, Yolanda went to the police station and filled out a victim of violent crime report, which meant that the state would pay for the entire funeral.

She also made the burial arrangements with William's Funerals and Rolling Hills, called all Slack's relatives, made him out to be a do-good daddy with the media, started a trust fund for the kids which received forty thousand in donations, and placed a ten-thousand-dollar bounty throughout the projects on the head of her husband's murderer. She would never have to pay off the bounty, but she didn't know that. All in all, Sheila was impressed by her girlfriend's strength.

Ironically, Yolanda spent the rest of her life as a martyr against violence, championing numerous causes along with serving as the unofficial ghetto voice in the war on drugs.

20
IT AIN'T OVER

Shakey sat on a top bunk in the bullpen still furious because of his arrest. He knew he hadn't killed anybody, so he felt like it was only a matter of time before his release.

He didn't know who killed Nadine but figured it must have been Big Ed or one of his flunkeys. The news of Slack's death hit him hard and left no doubt in his mind that Ed Tatum was behind it.

Sheila Rae proved her mettle by providing him with an indisputable alibi, so she was down for the count. He watched all the fellow inmates play dominoes, cards, checkers, and chess with little interest. His mind was on Big Ed and revenge.

The steel doors opened with the new prisoners entering. Shakey's attention was on the newscast sensationalizing the past week's murders. Glancing towards the door of the new arrivals he spotted Big Ed, who spotted him at the same time. Shakey hopped off his bunk, strode over to his rival, and stared him down.

Everyone scattered because the tension was so thick you could cut it with a knife. Without a word spoken between the two, it was on. . . .

Questions or comments, email Renay:
LADAYPUBLISHING@CS.COM

Thanks for your support!!

ABOUT THE AUTHOR

Renay Jackson is a former rapper and street lit author with five novels to his credit, all of which will be published by Frog, Ltd. over a two-year period. Jackson received the Chester Himes Black Mystery Writer Award in 2002. A single father to three daughters and a niece, he lives in Oakland, California, where he has been a custodian for the Oakland Police Department for more than twenty-five years.

Photo by Frank Alliger